Praise for VIRGINIA HAMILTON'S *The Gathering*

"Virginia Hamilton's artistry as an author is a pleasure to watch and to feel."

— *The Boston Globe*

The Gathering

Other Signature Editions by
VIRGINIA HAMILTON

Arilla Sun Down

Cousins

In the Justice Cycle:
Justice and Her Brothers (Book One)
Dustland (Book Two)

The Mystery of Drear House

Plain City

A White Romance

The Gathering

SCHOLASTIC INC.
New York Toronto London Auckland Sydney

If you purchased this book without a cover, you should be aware that this book is stolen property. It was reported as "unsold and destroyed" to the publisher, and neither the author nor the publisher has received any payment for this "stripped book."

ISBN 0-590-36216-X

12 11 10 9 8 7 6 5 4 3 2 1 8 9/9 0 1 2 3/0

Printed in the U.S.A. 01

First Scholastic printing, March 1998

Author photo by Jimmy Byrge

To my mother

Prologue

Leona Jefferson did her job, always. She was the Sensitive. Now she murmured incantations and placed spells in the long grass and snakebeds of the Quinella Trace lands. She followed the bank of the Quinella River to a great shade tree that grew thick with dark as the sun set.

"We waited for you," came the dreamy voice of Justice Douglass from under the tree.

The voice vibrated as the Sensitive knelt under branches. There were the four children of power seated around the shade buckeye. They had joined hands and were now the unit, ready to leave for the future.

"Wait!" cried the Sensitive, trying to hold them back.

Power filled the eyes of the four. *i am leaving,* the unit conveyed. *i will be back.*

The Sensitive sensed a calm farewell and a feeling of adventure as the unit went on its way.

i am the Watcher. The sounding rhythm of the unit vibrated.

An amazing light spread from the four. It tangled in piercing rays from the evening sun. Then the children were gone. However, their physical selves remained, hands joined around the tree.

The Sensitive waited out the lonely night. Softly she crooned to the empty-headed ones. She slept finally, sitting up. But her seer's insight stayed wide awake. Leona Jefferson missed nothing that was going on.

1

The unit was power. It had the force of four who were time-travelers. Now it was between its present and that future it knew as Dustland. It was in the Crossover between times. The Crossover echoed with sighs and whispers of mind-travelers trapped in it for eternity. Those travelers had failed to hold their concentration while mind-jumping from one time to another. They were trapped forever in the nowhere between times—unless, as swarming multi-beings, they grew powerful enough to will their way out. They attempted to capture new time-travelers, such as the unit on its way to Dustland.

The unit dared not lose concentration. It whirled, dodging t'being swarms. It massed its energy on the future and on a future animal it called Miacis. Its light was the Watcher, which surrounded the unit with clear purpose.

i am the Watcher, willed the unit.

The Watcher lit the way through the awful confusion the swarm placed in its way. At all cost, the unit must hold to its place and instant in the future.

It outmaneuvered vicious t'beings until it reached the final seam on the far side of the Crossover.

i am the Watcher, willed the unit. It rolled and plunged.

Future time started. The unit was there. At first it could not tell where it was. But gradually it divined that it had somehow entered the future within a dream that a being of Dustland had been having again and again. At once the unit lowered the level of its force so it might stay within the being's mind after the being awoke and the dream ended. For the unit was curious, interested in how swiftly the being had been learning since the coming of the dream.

This being was of innocent and simple mentality. It was not one of the three-legged Slaker humans, whom the unit had encountered before. It was two-legged, like the four of the unit. The unit would help the being. He was a youth, stunted in growth but skilled in survival. His name was Duster. The unit would give Duster all the help it could. And it stayed hidden in the unconscious

Duster while an entity known as Mal came and went and the boy slept.

Duster wiggled in the five-foot-long hole that was his *dark*, the den he had made for himself before Graylight's end. He did not awaken. Dead tired from the Graylight's roam, his weary muscles finally relaxed their tension.

A youth known as Siv, the leggens, was asleep in his own *dark* to one side of Duster. Nearer Duster on his left side in another *dark* was one called Glass, the smooth-keep. Glass was lovely, the color of honey. She was tiny, barely four feet tall; yet she had superior skill, and Duster admired her greatly.

Duster was the leader. He was the leader for a packen of fifteen youngens. The youngens were divided into five trips of three youngens each. The best was that Duster was Siv and Glass's leader. The three of them were the most skilled trip in all of the roamer packens. This was the reason Duster could sleep soundly and why he could dream without fear. Old Siv on his right would never allow anything to harm him. And the smooth, gentle Glass was as swift and soundless as any fighter and thrower in the packens. The best.

Neither Siv nor Glass appeared in the dream Duster had over and over again. On the edges of the dream moved something golden, traveling swiftly. But when the dream began, there was the tone of Siv's voice being playful, also commanding. The sound of it was loud and magnified. Duster never could hear clearly enough to understand what Siv was singing. There was just the teasing, commanding tone. A strange, out-of-place tone, since Siv never commanded. Then Duster heard a crowd responding, humming their understanding. Once or twice the crowd cried out in fear.

Slowly the dream made Duster uneasy. He had the notion that he must find old Siv and silence him forever. And in the dream his view was from behind his own back, just as if he were smooth Glass at his elbow. Glass stayed at his elbow when they roamed, keeping their arsenal of weapons at the ready. At Duster's left arm, she could easily slip a *pound* into his hand.

In an attack they never stopped moving. Only when Graylight ended, at the time of Nolight, did they stop to dig their *dark* dens for a few hours' rest and sleeping. When it was Graylight, they stayed in one place long enough to kill and to eat.

Duster could heave a pound force farther than most. But he was leader, his job was to command. He left all throwing to Glass. Siv, who was taller than Duster, could outrun most animals that trailed the packen by day. Siv could outrun every human of their land except good Glass. But Glass refused to be the leggens. Glass did what she wanted. She could kill close in, if she had to, swiftly with her deep-daggen. She could hurl a *sharp* or a *shot* seventy paces with no loss of accuracy, killing smoothly.

Glass despised killing of any kind, in defense of packen or trip, or for food. But she would do the deed if Duster commanded her to, and without an instant's hesitation. She knew Duster would not give such a command unless it was necessary. Glass trusted his judgment, and that made him proud.

For some time Duster slept deeply. Then he surfaced to dream. He dreamed the presence of the smooth behind him on his left. Glass muttered a singsong under her breath, as she would do when there was danger.

Dreaming, he toned lightly over his shoulder, "Quiet, smooth Glass! In no time we be gone."

Suddenly all notion of her, of having her skill at his back, left him. Glass no longer existed.

In his dreaming the playful, commanding voice of Siv ceased abruptly. All was silence. Duster felt Siv slip past him on his left. That would be something the leggens would never do, Duster dreamed, something Duster would never permit. For the left side of the leader belonged to the smooth-keep. Then Siv, too, was gone from the dream. Yet the mocking impression of him remained with Duster.

Dreaming, Duster followed a hard, sleek surface. Such a road was impossible in his land of shifting dust. But as soon as he felt it under his feet, he knew the name of it—triway. Duster was at home on the road of the triway. High above him, the way had two more levels, which disappeared at the limits of his eyesight. Supports like silver threads held the upper levels in place. The supports glowed in all-too-familiar dim light.

Dreaming, suddenly there was bright day. Fresh air. Duster was glad to be alive. Here was a land of beauty, with dwelling places arranged in patterns that were pleasing. One of them would be fine for him to live in. But Duster had no place to live—that was why he was on the low level of the triway, which was on the ground. The way moved along on its own, but Duster moved faster.

"Be running," he toned, dreaming.

He heard a wim's voice over a speaker. "Suntime," she trilled. "You have forty-five beats in your favor. Enjoy."

Sunlight spilled over Duster. "Turn it down!" He shielded his eyes from the burning light and kept running.

"Be running," Duster toned. "Catch me, nothing!"

Something startling occurred right before his eyes. It was the four with power out of the present materializing in Duster's dream.

Four strangers came toward him along the way. They were one too many for a youngen trip and far too few for a packen. They hurried toward Duster. One of them, the wim with dark, curly hair, touched him and took hold of his hand.

"Be touching leader, wrong." His toning lacked command. He knew it, but did nothing to make the wim take her hand from his.

"We must hide here," she said in a grating voice. "Oh, Duster, please let us stay in your dream."

Such bright light was in her eyes! Such strength in her soundings! She made no warring tones to trouble him. Duster found that he was delighted to have them with him.

"Stay here," he told them. "Rest by the triway, but out of sight. I be on the run myself."

"We know," they said in one voice. "This is more than dream. It is also memory of what was. Don't worry. We will protect your thoughts."

All at once Duster awoke in his *dark*. Knowledge of the four talking to him in his dream was locked away before he was fully awake. What Duster knew was that he'd been dreaming for a long time; he had been caught in the dream, taken somewhere. By whom, he didn't know. But he was filled with dread. The feeling didn't go away when he realized that the smooth-keep leaned over him. Roughly she picked the dirt from his hair.

Duster saw that it was a new Graylight in his land where there was never much more than shade, except for dawn, when Graylight sparkled. Duster had always felt good about his land until the dreaming began coming to him. Now he who was leader felt saddened.

His lean, muscled shoulders sagged, causing him to seem smaller than his nearly five-foot height. This worry bothered the smooth, Glass, for it distracted her leader. It upset the leggens, Siv, who had now taken his position facing the leader on Duster's right.

Siv didn't move a muscle. He waited for the ritual between leader and smooth-keep to be completed.

"So the dawn be over?" Duster toned to the smooth. "Why you not be singing out the Graylight, then?"

Duster asked the same few questions every Graylight. Questions made Siv impatient. Yet, good leggens that he was, he stood his ground. He went into himself, which was the polite thing to do during the process of shaking dirt and dust out.

Glass pulled Duster from his *dark.* He stood with dirt and dust covering him.

"You look the fool," Glass summed up.

"But will the dawn be gone?" Duster toned. He loved seeing the lights of dawn.

"Oh, certainly, you know," she sang out. "What be in your brain—more dust?"

"Oh, rough Smooth!" Duster moaned. "Be so hard on my poor self."

"Hahn!" sung impatiently, was all she felt like answering back.

Although smaller than Duster, Glass was nearly as muscled. And covered with dust the same as he, it would have been difficult for others to know which was which, Siv observed.

The leggens had already taken care of his first-light ritual. He had done his moves—soft art leverages, flips and presses, running in place, handstands—which shook loose most of the dirt from his *dark.* With leather mitts he had brushed off the remainder. He had fashioned mitts for the smooth and for the leader, too. Siv had no desire to be close-in the way leader and smooth were. He stood alone, needed no close-in. Leggens was what he was; he was content.

Duster and Glass put on their mitts. They began to smack each other gently about the face and arms. Halfway through, Glass boxed Duster strongly about the ears.

"Be joking too fast," Duster toned. "Stop it, Glass."

"Who be joking? Be brushing you off," she hummed.

"You call that brushing?" Duster trilled. "I call you hurting."

"You be a big fool, then." She clipped him hard under the chin.

Neat score, thought Siv. The leader not be letting that pass.

Duster gave Glass a hard smack to the jaw. She returned with a jarring kick to his rump.

Swiftly he caught her foot in one hand and swung her off the ground. Then he had her by both feet.

"Ha-hahn!" he toned in triumph, disturbing to nearby trips who had been sleeping still.

"Noisy Duster!" someone shouted a three-tone, signaling no offense at cautioning the leader.

"Fill his mouth with dirt," came a fighting singsong from someone else.

Duster ignored them and swung the smooth-keep around and around by her feet. Her arms were straight out in front of her, with the palms of her hands touching. Duster knew that any moment she would flip sideways and spin free. Before she could execute the move, he let go of her feet. Glass went flying over the dust. Small and agile, she managed to tuck her legs and head before she hit the ground in a curl. Glass rolled nicely, but the impact knocked the breath out of her. She shivered on her back, her mouth agape with the pain.

Duster was beside her. He bent over her, smiling. "Don't be testing the leader before his food-time," sounding in his well-modulated command mode.

In a moment, when Glass had her breath again, she grew formal with her leader. She got to her feet and stood at attention. Careful to hold back anger from her tone, she sounded, "It be my mistake, O Duster. Lead on."

With palms down, Duster crossed his wrists, dismissing her. He gave away not one single tone. Leader, he was.

Glass turned on her heel and took her stand to the left of Siv, the leggens. They now had their backs to Duster.

Duster gazed at their rigid pose and nodded with satisfaction at the strength they held between them loyal Siv and smooth Glass. No leader could ask for better first- and sec-sides at his command. He murmured a six-tone of thanks, taking his place in front of them with his back to them, Siv on his right and Glass on his left.

Shortly after, Glass burst out with a fighting singsong: "The beasts be running!"

Her arm and leg muscles tensed in preparation. Likely she would not need to rescue the leggens, but if old Siv got into trouble, Glass would defend him. Only when Siv missed the first weapon thrust, or if he was attacked, would the smoothkeep dare leave her leader's left side.

"Go then, good Siv," Duster toned over his shoulder. "Hunger be making me twitch. Be second day hungering. Go, before we weaken."

"I'm gone!" rumbled Siv with a deep and daring tone.

His long, slender legs glided gracefully into the murk of Dustland.

2

Hunger propelled a beast into a self-weapon. Duster spied it streaking toward Siv, the leggens. Motionless, Siv was barely visible in the distance. Then he was moving, running. He raised one arm straight up, signaling to the leader and smooth-keep that he had sighted the deadly beast.

Glass's face froze in concentration as she peered toward Siv.

Duster took two side steps to his right, in front of the place Siv had been. By this move he gave the smooth-keep room to throw. Glass had both hands behind and just below her neck, ready to thrust them into the pack she carried between her shoulder blades. With lightning speed she could pull weapons from her pack and set them in motion. The moment Siv leaped high and spun toward her, she would release the weapon an arm movement from him had signaled.

Now, in the distance, Duster sighted two

pumps of Siv's right arm. And softly he toned to Glass to make ready the deep-daggen.

Glass found the bone weapon by feel, pulling it expertly from the pack. The deep-daggen was hollow and weighted with grit and dirt that was sealed inside.

"Now!" Duster toned, his voice loud.

Glass threw with strength and accuracy. The heaving motion was so smooth, Duster found it impossible to tell when she released the daggen. But he saw it disappear in the murk.

Instantly, it seemed, Siv had the daggen in his grasp and raised it for the leader and smooth to see. It was a bit whiter than the gray light of day. Moving still, Siv timed his run away from the beast so it overtook him at the moment of its most furious stride. The beast had no chance to leap. It must run to kill, leaning ever closer toward the leggens.

The animal was at full speed. It could do nothing when, with an added burst of momentum, a powerful second wind, the leggens crossed in front of it, out of reach.

Be perfect move! Duster observed. Now the leggens' weapon hand holding the deep-daggen was nearest the animal.

Siv slashed from the beast's rump forward along its spine. It was still running when its backbone split in two. More slashes with the daggen separated flesh and skin from the split spinal column. The animal's legs buckled. With a loud crack it nosed into the dust, its neck broken.

The beast died. Siv knelt beside it and carved a clean line across its withers. Watchful that no other beast take him by surprise, Siv worked the skin down the body. He cut it away and stashed it inside out at the bottom of his catchen bag. A wild, warm odor rose from the animal flesh. His stomach heaved with the good smell of it.

Be food for all! Siv made a mental note. Leader be glad.

Before the animal flesh could cool, he carved it, placing bloody chunks on top of the skin at the bottom of his catchen. Then Siv hacked the ribcage and shank bones into manageable parts. He stuffed them along the insides of the catchen. Finally he loped back to his trip

Siv sang out, "Leader, I win by your luck," trotting up to Duster. He laid his catchen at Duster's feet, opening it and spreading out the kill. He toned a rejoicing and handed over the kill daggen.

Duster licked the blood on the deep-daggen. He touched the signs of his own good sorceru carved on it by his own hand. Then he pressed the daggen to Siv's right arm in thanks. "Good Siv!" he toned. "Leggens be true!"

Siv grinned and, with respect, did not touch the leader.

Glass then sang out a trilling of her own thanks. Her cool voice was well modulated. Clear and clean, it had a crystal quality in the thick air. Duster found her voice as thirst-quenching as a palm of fresh water. When she finished her song, he touched the daggen with his sorceru to her left arm, giving thanks for her part in the kill. Duster handed her the deep-daggen for her to sharpen again and put away.

There had been a large run of beasts, as Duster had suspected there would be. His plan had been to situate his packen of youngens between a freshwater pool he'd come upon in a place where no water had ever been, and the trail wandering beasts might take when they scented the pool.

Since he had begun dreaming, Duster had learned to plan ahead, and had even thought to wonder how the water pool came to be. He didn't know how dreaming helped him question or learn new things. He simply knew that it must. So much that was new now happened within him. And he felt overjoyed with the growing in his head.

Packens of youngens seemed never to learn that beasts must always come to water. Youngens and even the grims, who were older and roamed in their own packs, did not understand why humans covered themselves with dirt in the *dark* dens. Duster knew. It was to keep moisture in themselves, absorbing what little moisture there was from the dirt. Duster was beginning to realize much. He taught new tones of voice that he made easy for Siv and Glass to learn. They accepted what he taught them. He was leader. Siv thought every leader learned to teach and to dream as his leader did, so he expressed to Duster. But Duster knew they did not.

Three leggens of the packen trotted forward, laying their catchens by Siv's. Each bent forward before Duster. Duster took their weapons and tasted the blood. He noted that the signs of their lesser leaders' sorceru were good. He pressed their weapons to their right arms, just as he had done with his Siv's.

The smooth-keeps of the packen came forward. Duster repeated the gesture of thanks he had given to Glass.

Leggens and smooth-keeps stood in line behind Duster's Siv and Glass as leaders of trips came forward. Duster gave to each a personal tone of regard. Each, in turn, gave him a nod with head turned away and a tone of awe given only to the leader of packen. Duster accepted the awe due his authority.

So it was that there was calm in the packen. All had been given full share in Duster's praise of them for food-time. Now the packen formed up to eat. Trip leaders and Duster made the center group. The leggens with Siv formed the inner circle. The smooth-keeps under Glass had the outside, in which they turned away from the center to guard both leggens and leaders from danger.

Food was slashed into serving portions by the leggens' circle. Bled pouches were handed over to the leggens so blood from the kills could be squeezed into them. Later they would go as a packen to the fresh-water pool to drink as much as they wanted. Food was passed into the leaders' circle and out to the smooth-keeps'. All ate, savoring the delicious taste of wildmeat.

While they ate, the entity called Mal came, sweeping across the land at the level of the dust. Leggens threw down their food, feeling nauseous, heads aching. Smooth-keeps recognized the power of the unseen force that hurt the leggens. They saw and heard nothing with which to do battle. Angry, they felt a sickening fear. They spilled their bled pouches in the dust. Weapons were useless. The smooths covered their eyes and fell to their knees.

Duster stood in his circle of leaders. He had awareness. Always he had it for the unseen nonbeing. Only with the coming of his dreaming had he known to think of It as Mal. The Mal. Mal, as if he had forever called It so.

Leaders shielded their eyes, as if the fear and sickness Mal brought them could cause blindness.

Standing there, Duster sensed the Mal sweeping back and forth, making most of them deathly ill and afraid. To Duster, Mal was like Nolight and Graylight. It came and went. It was, is, to be endured.

"What it be you seeking?" toned Duster to the Mal.

The leaders shuddered. Complete dark of Mal descended to surround the packen.

Not you, spoke the Mal. *I seek others. Have you felt others?*

"Be seeing no others," Duster toned, feeling simple-minded, unthinking. He recognized himself as the old Duster with nothing much in his mind.

If others do come, you will tell me at once? asked the Mal.

"Yes," the old Duster said simply, believing he would.

What is it you wish?

"Be wishing for nothing," Duster toned.

All is well here?

"Well being," toned Duster.

This land is your place, said the Mal.

"Be knowing that," softly now Duster toned, serene.

You will not leave . . . you will not try again to leave?

"Once be trying," sang Duster. "You be making me so sick, I quit."

Do others think to try?

"Only leggens ever be thinking it," trilled Duster. "Be come sickness and almost dying. Leggens never even be thinking it again!"

All is well, then?

"All," toned Duster.

The Mal swept on, taking away the utter dark. Leggens felt better and began to eat again. The smooth-keeps were upset because their bled pouches lay dusty on the ground. They would not be able to clean the pouches until the packen went for water. They must try to be more careful, they told one another. Duster toned to them not to worry. The smooths brightened. Soon they forgot that the Mal had come.

This time of the Mal, Duster had been made into the old Duster of slow thoughts. The Mal thought nothing had changed. Duster realized this and was not afraid. Now he remembered that in his dreaming there had come a wonder. Within the dream, but not a part of it, he remembered seeing four strangers who came toward him along the way. They had hurried to him—how had he forgotten? The wim had touched him and spoken words to him. He remembered there had been no troubling tones in her voice.

Duster still stood in his group of leaders as the packen continued its food-time. Now, happily he trilled in his resounding tenor voice:

"Come out. Be come out from my head, wherever my dream be waiting to dream. You, travelers, be come out. Come out! The Mal be gone!"

The unit mind-jumped free from Duster. Truly the Mal was gone. The unit took on form, but kept itself invisible from Duster and his packen so it would not cause another disturbance so soon after the Mal. It settled its force away from the smoothkeeps' circle. It knew it must go slowly. It must not frighten Duster.

With a delicate probe it summoned Duster to bring Glass and Siv before it.

Duster touched Siv, signaling the leggens to follow him. When he came to Glass's circle, he took her by the hand, pulling her to her feet. Surely she could feel his trembling. It didn't concern him that she might think him afraid. He had no time now to tone to her and explain.

The power out of his dream was unlike what Duster knew the Mal to be. He had seen the power in the shape of four separate youngens. They were human, like him, but taller, even taller than the leggens. They could be four thoughts as separate as the humans he had seen, or they could be one thought and one mind. The awareness of such strange power terrified Duster. He shook all over in anticipation of what might come.

Another Mal? he wondered. He did not think so. Then, what?

The force of power was near the ground in front of the packen. Duster felt it observe, listening.

He formed up his trip in its proper order. Glass was behind him on his left; Siv, on his right.

"Why this way we be up?" Glass toned. "Be wanting my meat." She had not finished eating.

With a hand behind his back, Duster gave her a circling thumb signal to keep still. Glass read him. Still she couldn't understand why she had been taken away from her circle while eating.

"Why be we this standing?" she toned.

"Be straight!" Duster commanded in a deadly tone.

"Am straight!" Glass responded instantly. She toned a triad of duty, attention and respect. There was an undertone of apology for breaking the leader's order-of-trip.

"Be straight!" Duster toned to Siv.

"Am straight!" At rigid attention, the leggens toned on one note, showing that he need make no apology.

"Be ready!" Duster toned hotly, pitching the sound deep in the low register.

"*Am* ready!" Glass trilled.

"*Am* ready!" Siv toned in a crisp burst of melody.

"Be still!" Duster sang in his pure tenor. It held such manly force, his packen stopped the last sucking of bones and licking of fingers.

Siv, Glass and the packen made no reply to Duster's final command. They were now at easy attention. From his tone, they understood he had a message for them. And he began singing a plain-song for them. It was a free-rhythm melody.

To the packen: "Pay attention, all."

To Siv and Glass: "There comes a fine knowing. Be afraid, nothing."

To his trip and packen:

"Be strong. Open heads, let in knowing.
    Knowing,
Be trying it.
O packen! O smooth and leggens!
This be the one. Be some Graylight,
Knowing!"

Duster's voice quavered. But it found its true strength again as the plainsong ended.

The packen trilled. It used contralto, soprano, tenor and bass ranges in a swift changing from chest-voice to head-voice and falsetto. If Duster's singing could inspire, the packen's could mesmerize. The meaning of its hushed trilling was quite clear to the unit listening.

"We be sure of you, O Duster," the packen intoned. "We be straight at your command. Lead on."

At the head of trip and packen, Duster waited. The stillness, the murk gathered around him. They all waited patiently for what would come.

3

The unit separated into four minds. Justice, her brothers, Levi and Thomas, and their friend Dorian Jefferson became their individual selves. Justice was the Watcher and the balance for the unit's strength. Brother Thomas was the magician who could cloud minds with marvelous and terrible illusions. And he longed to have Justice's gift of greatest power. Levi was the caring, kind brother. He was not physically strong and had only a limited gift of telepathy. Their pal Dorian was known as healer among them.

It was a half-hour before the four allowed themselves visibility before Duster and his packen.

Thomas was shivering; he tried to shake off the effect of such awesome singing. The vocalizing of Duster and his tribe had touched them all deeply. They were moved by the bravery of these children in the face of unseen power.

It had stunned Justice the way they communicated through vocalizing. And they lived without grown-ups, with the bare minimum for survival.

Using telepathy, she traced to her brothers and Dorian, *Think of the grown-ups, the grims! Off somewhere by themselves, I guess. We could find out more from Duster's thoughts.*

She was eager to see grown-ups. All at once she thought about her folks and felt the pain of longing.

No, I won't go home yet. Not now.

Justice wore a hooded robe, socks and sandals. The boys were dressed similarly in hooded tunics and comfortable trousers. Absently she touched her arms and feet, the clothing. They felt just as real in Dustland as they did at home in the present. She sighed, forcing her mind away from what was and was not possible here in the future.

They're no bigger than eleven-year-olds! Thomas traced, about the packen.

You'd be that little, too, if you had to starve all your life, Dorian traced back.

Well, you saw 'em bring down those animals. Mostly small beasties, Thomas traced, *but still food. And they ate it* raw!

But how often do you think they find so much food? Justice traced. *Not every day, I bet. Maybe only once a month.*

Nobody can live eating just once a month, Levi traced.

They might learn to, Justice answered. *They lived without water, with only the liquid from animals they killed, before we made the water pool for them.*

Are they all really eleven-year-olds? Dorian interrupted.

They're fifteen, Justice traced. *I read that from Duster's mind. They're all approximately the same age.*

They'd have to be the same age, wouldn't they? Levi traced. He was staring at the packen with a mixture of disbelief and revulsion.

Huh? Thomas was the last to see. There was quiet in which they waited for him; they had already seen. A long moment, then Thomas seemed to gather himself in.

It can't be! he traced. *I don't believe it!*

Well, believe it, it's true, Justice traced. *The packen youngens are duplicates of either Duster, Siv or Glass.*

They were exact replicas. Thomas could see that when he looked beyond the dust and dirt covering them. There were four Dusters, four Sivs and four Glasses seated in the group. Counting the Duster, Siv and Glass who were standing, there were five of each kind, one of each kind of duplicate in every trip.

I don't believe it, Thomas traced again, like a whisper.

We'd better show ourselves, Justice traced back.

Wait, he traced. *What are they? Somebody knows how to make people just alike here?*

I don't think so. Not here in Dustland, she traced.

Then there is an outside!

We knew there had to be, else why would the Slaker beings try to find an end to Dustland? Levi traced.

When I saw them Slakers with their wings and three legs, I said this place had to be a zoo!

And I said it was a prison, Justice traced.

Thomas nodded. *I think you're right. But who put the Slakers and Duster and them here? What have they done?*

We'll have to find that out, she traced. *Come, we'd better get on with it.*

Gradually the four became visible. They were at first separate columns of shade. The columns took on form, shape and color. With coloration came depth and dimension. They became solid, real.

A shudder rippled over the packen. Youngens uttered tones of alarm. Sharp and quick were the soundings. What had been three circles of leaders, leggens and smooth-keeps was now a tight clump of frightened children. They huddled close, touching hands for comfort.

At the sight of the four with power, Glass faltered, stumbling into Duster's back. Siv nearly jumped out of his skin. Unashamedly they held Duster's hands tightly.

Glass toned to Duster in a thin, little voice: "Who be them things?"

She had broken Duster's command for quiet. He forgave her this time, so overwhelming was the moment. He toned excitedly, "Glass, be waiting for leader to settle it."

"But who be them shadow things, Leader?" she toned.

"They be tight with us, Glass, I be sure of it," he toned.

Justice smiled at them. "Be tight with you, O Duster," she sang out in her best voice, startling the packen and Duster and his trip.

Justice's voice had always been musical. With a little effort, she had come close enough to the right toning to make herself understood.

Carefully Duster came forward to stand before her. "We be tight, then," he toned, in a fine tremolo of hauteur signifying his leadership. He hand-signaled his trip to be at ease. Siv and Glass had taken a fighting stance—legs apart, arms swinging free—but they came forward now behind their leader.

Duster placed his hands on Justice's shoulders. He would have lowered his head on his right hand, had she not been nearly as tall as he. To each of the boys also he made this gesture of tightening.

"Be tight, you," he toned with a fine feeling of caring. "Be tight, me."

Glass and Siv touched each boy's chest with their heads. It was as high as their heads reached and their way of taking part in tightening. Despite an extreme effort of self-control, they cringed at contact with such odd-smelling, tall beings.

The packen duplicates hugged one another.

Dorian and Thomas giggled at the packen's queer behavior. The youngens took part in the tightening by connecting with themselves!

"These be in my dream," Duster toned, explaining the appearance of the four to his trip and packen.

Siv nodded. Glass looked confused.

"We came here through Duster's dream," Justice half-spoke, half-sang in her clearest voice. "We come from far to join you, if you will let us."

"You be trip—one, two, three and one?" toned Glass. "How be two the same?"—motioning toward the identical twins, Thomas and Levi. And staring at Justice and Dorian, she toned, "You, one-two, be something else."

"I see what you mean." Justice spoke this time.

"Well, I don't," Thomas muttered. He did not stutter as he did at home. He never stuttered when they were in Dustland or when tracing through telepathy.

The packen set up a furious chattering beneath their breath whenever one of the four spoke. It was beginning to annoy Thomas. *Shut up, you clowns*! he traced.

"Glass means that there are two of us, not five that look alike," Justice was explaining. "And if we were a trip, none of us would look alike. But we have one too many for a trip, and just two who look alike."

"So?" Thomas said.

"Well, she finds it curious, that's all," Justice said. "Weird, I guess, for her to see Dorian and me with no more like us."

All at once Glass kicked dust in Justice's face, catching Thomas in the face also. She moved so swiftly, they could not shield themselves.

"Why, you—" Thomas sputtered.

"Cold on you two!" Dorian shouted, laughing. "Ooh, cold on you guys!"

Glass was a little thing, but lithe and strong. She looked just like a fifteen-year-old girl in miniature. Such a little one, bravely kicking dust in the face of power! That was what Dorian found so funny.

Without warning, Duster swung on Glass. The blow wasn't vicious. It was hard, purposeful. It knocked her unconscious to the ground.

"Don't!" Levi grabbed Duster's arm.

Duster pulled loose. "Be touching leader, wrong!" His eyes glinted like sunlight on ice. He sang fortissimo in an ominous minor tone.

"Look! Look!" Dorian pointed at the packen. Every trip leader had swung on every smooth-keep, knocking them out cold.

"Oh, wow!" said Levi, turning away.

"You want to join up with these clowns?" Thomas asked Justice.

Justice didn't answer. There was silence in which the Watcher rose in a glow in her eyes. Power rising. All understood words she implanted in each of them.

O Duster, this is no way to begin. Tell me my mistakes.

Through her, Duster's thoughts were revealed to all.

Duster explained: Glass be saying why you a trip, one, two, three and one. You be singing back nothing. She be fighting over that. And leader be not letting a smooth-keep fight any tightening.

It was my fault, Justice traced.

Fault? Duster thought.

No, nothing. Why did you strike Glass? Justice traced.

Glass be not on her own, fighting. Glass be doing what the leader commands.

Oh, I see. So are we still a tightening?

Be still one.

You can call me Justice, she traced.

Justice, thought Duster.

And call him Thomas, and him Levi, and the last one you can call Dorian.

Thomas . . . Levi, Duster thought. Dorian.

Good! That's it, traced Justice. *Those are our names. We know your names, too. You're Duster. And that's Siv and over there is Glass.*

Glass was coming to. At the sound of her name, she got up carefully and took her place at Duster's left side. In the packen, also, smooth-keeps were up and in their circle.

Calm settled over trip and packen. Glass and Duster toned quietly to one another. A thoughtful Siv took in every shade of meaning.

"She be a strong thing," Glass toned to Duster. "Be not easy, fighting."

"You be not fighting. She be a leader," he toned.

"Leader be better that one." She gazed at Thomas.

"Be more than one leader?" toned Siv, with a trill of apology for intruding. "She be leader and Thomas one be leader?"

"And three be smooth-keep and one be leg-gens?" Glass sang out.

"That be it," softly Duster toned. "One, two, three, one."

Smiling at them, Justice spoke in calm tones. "We are like a trip, but being one, two, three and one, we are called a unit. We can be separate the way Duster is separate from Siv and from Glass. You are a trip. We are a unit. We care to join the packen. Join like a trip, but as a unit. Maybe sometime another one with us. Another one is called Miacis. An animal, Miacis. Having four legs."

A clamoring arose in the packen. Glass took her fighting stance. Siv was loose, one foot before the other, ready to run an evasive action on command. Duster was poised in silence, ready to do in an instant what must be done.

"My mistake to talk of this golden animal, Miacis," Justice said in a soothing voice. "We wish to travel with you, O Duster, we of the unit. We can be our own trip with you and the packen."

It interested Duster, these tones and levels of pitch the wim out of his dream could tone. And it amused him how terrible her voice could be when it slipped off key. The voice had few pitches that did not, at one time or another, grate on his thinking. Yet he understood her. And now he was silent, wondering about these strange ones who had come from far, yet had walked in from his dreaming.

An animal, she had said. A beast, part of her unit.

Duster thought and thought. Recalled a golden thing in his dreaming, streaking across the land. She had said a golden animal. Whatever kind was the golden animal from his dreaming, it was not a kind for the leggens to bring down on a run. That kind, golden, filled Duster with caring for it. Dreaming, he heard it bark what sounded like words from the distance.

"Who be you four humans?" Duster toned. His voice was strong in its leader's mode.

"We are friends from far past," Justice said.

"Friends? Be what, friends? I know no past," toned Duster.

"Friends are those who support you, come to travel with you," Justice said. "The far past is our time frame. We come from past—was—to this that is your now."

"Friends, nothing," coldly Duster toned. "Was, nothing."

He tested the atmosphere of the four. It did not give off a bad feeling, but he must make certain.

"You be some kind of Mal, then?" Duster toned.

The four looked startled. They stared long and hard at one another, but made no sound that Duster could hear. He laughed inwardly, for these had shown that they need not make sound. They could plant thinking within one another, anyone.

"You be using mindsong," he toned at them,

proud that he'd found a way to describe their private thinking.

They were startled again, and this made Duster laugh.

"That's a good way to put it," Justice said. "You know of the Mal by name," she said carefully. "Mal is a friend that supports you?"

"I know the Mal," Duster toned easily.

"The Mal came to our time frame," she said.

"It be bringing you here?" Duster toned in a voice like flint.

"Mal tried to keep us from coming," Justice said. "It would fight us to keep us away from here. We came anyway. We want to find a way for Slaker beings to get out of here. They want so much to go."

Duster held himself still, alert inside. He searched their faces, then turned to his packen and Siv and Glass. He must not make a mistake now. And it was some time before he made a move. A long kind of time, facing the four, while in his mind he sorted out what was known. He had helped the four hide in his dream. Was it Mal they hid from? Probably it was they who had kept the Mal from discovering his learning mind. As far as Duster could understand, the four had done no harm.

He raised his fist above his head; he let his arm fall, pointing to the ground, and began a plainsong.

"Be going, getting out of this place," he toned. "Getting away, knowing which way, oh, long before anyone. Oh, very small Duster being. So few of my years; never this fifteen of my years. More like eight or nine, tough Duster. Here be me and other youngens one Graylight and not knowing where be me or them the Graylight before. So many Graylights trying to know and running with youngens."

"O Duster. O Leader!" intoned the packen.

"Be running every which way," sang Duster.

"Be running *one which way*, come be feeling so bad. Getting me deep. Knowing be the way out and be wanting to go out, eagerly. And be running that way, me and some youngens. Sickness coming fast. So sickening, make us be backing our tracks. Be falling down. Be lying down, so sick. Never get me up.

"And the Mal be come, singing to me. *Duster will not run away?*

"Be telling Mal, 'Only try, why not be trying?'

"And the Mal making me so sick, saying *Duster will never run away?*

"Be singing to the Mal, if It be leaving sickness outta me, never me be run away again.

"Mal saying, 'Then you lead youngens from sickness. All ways lead them back. No run away.' "

"O Duster! O Leader!" intoned the packen.

"Poor youngens," sang Siv and Glass.

"Grims finding us," Duster toned simply. "Olders be helping youngens. Then be throwing us away when we be a few more of our years."

Duster's song came to an end. Now he knelt on one knee, with the other beneath his chin and his arms wrapped around it. He stared vacantly before him. Siv and Glass stretched out on their stomachs on either side of him. They made piles of dust and thrust their hands into them. The three of them watched Justice and her brothers and Dorian Jefferson.

Their at-ease postures meant that they would trust the four completely, Justice realized. Silently she regarded them when Dorian began tracing.

So that's how they got here, he traced.

How? Thomas traced back. *All we know is that one day Duster found himself here with some others, with no memory of where they'd been before. The Mal said they had to stay. So they formed a tribe. A pack.*

Are they made to stay here because they're duplicates? Dorian traced.

Who knows? traced Thomas. *Duster doesn't even seem surprised that the others look just like him. Maybe it's like when I look at Levi. It's like looking at myself.*

Then, in a quiet, respectful tone, Justice asked Duster, "When will Mal come again?"

"When Mal comes," Duster replied.

"Mal must not know we are with Duster's packen," she said. She had divined that Duster would permit them to travel with his tribe. "We will hide Levi, Thomas and Dorian in a trip," she said. "I will not be seen by you or anyone, but I will be with you."

All of this Justice enveloped in a mist of daydreams, in case the Mal had some way of staying in contact with Duster's mind.

Sleepily Duster followed the daydreams. Siv and Glass had the daydreams and did not wonder about them; they accepted them, knew them.

A while after, Duster got to his feet. He stretched this way and that, getting the stiffness out, for he'd knelt on one knee for some time. He pulled himself up straight in his leader's pose. "Be making our way. Water now," he toned.

The leggens and smooth-keep got up, ready and waiting. The packen responded, forming into trips—leader, leggens, smooth-keep. In seconds all were in position. Duster waited for the unit to arrange itself.

The three boys took up positions at the center of the packen. They slouched as low as was comfortable.

"I don't think the Mal checks Duster's packen every day," Justice said, "but to be safe, stay low."

"We could become invisible again," Levi said.

"That would upset the packen worse than

seeing you with them," she said. "They might feel something close to them and get frightened. Then Mal would know something for sure. Stay low. I'll ride with one of you."

Before disappearing from sight, Justice suggested to Duster and the others that she was there with them. She mind-traced to them that they need not worry about her again.

The boys didn't know which of them had Justice with him. And not knowing, they could keep their thoughts as simple as those of the youngens.

She made herself as small as a germ. Microscopic through the power of her will, she rode in a dust particle under the hood of Levi's tunic.

Her mind raced with the wonder of Duster, his tribe and trip. They shouldn't be in this place, she thought. If there's a way out, I'll find it. Is my purpose here to save them? I'm sensing there's more to it, but maybe that's the first step.

4

The odor of the packen surrounded them. Thomas felt just the way he did when he'd watched too much television—cranky, jumpy, overtired. He knew very well he couldn't be trudging through the heat and dust of some awful future time and place. But he was, and with Dorian and Levi on either side of him.

With Justice hidden, Thomas realized he was now the leader of Dorian and Levi. He was the one they would depend on, and he cautioned himself to stay alert. And yet the dreamlike pace they kept, the sameness of the packen, was hypnotic. No matter where Thomas looked, he saw another Siv, another Glass and Duster. It got monotonous, but it was oddly exciting, too.

Thomas scanned the minds of the group. The Glass ones' keenest thoughts were their trust in and protection of the leaders, Thomas discovered.

Leggens ones tended toward moodiness. They were all aloof, independent and as highstrung as runners could be.

Thomas envied Duster's position of high esteem given him by his trip and his packen and, he supposed, even by the other roamer packens. There *were* other packens. Thomas had divined that by telepathy. He could send his mind out swiftly, intercepting thoughts of packens just out of sight of this one.

Given him—or did he take it? Thomas wondered, about Duster's position of high esteem. I bet I could beat Duster in a fair fight, he thought. You can tell he's no fighter, if he leaves combat up to a *girl!* What's he for, then?

Thomas felt a familiar telepathy enter his mind. It was Dorian. *Couldn't help picking up what you were thinking. Nothing much else to do. But I figure Duster's singing is what he can do.*

Yeah, traced Thomas, *but what good is singing in a place like Dustland?*

Well, he can lead to water, too, Dorian traced.

Yeah, Duster knows the way to water, all right, Thomas traced. For he had divined they were headed directly for the water pool.

Soon they began to feel the moisture from the pool. It mixed with the dust in a slippery film, like oil and talc, and they were soon covered with it.

Uh-uh! Thomas thought. I haven't got a body here. There's nothing but my thoughts.

But he did have a body, no denying what he could see and feel. And now he looked much like any member of the packen.

Out of boredom, Thomas entered the mind of the Siv nearest him. Mind-jumping was quite different from telepathic tracing. It was like walking through the walls of a large hall full of unexpected clutter, sometimes unimaginable treasure. Wherever Thomas entered, he at once owned it and could do with it whatever he wanted. Thomas could mind-jump and control anyone except his sister, and the Sensitive Mrs. Jefferson back home, whose power was stronger than his.

Inside the Siv, Thomas felt he was looking down a dusty tunnel. The view centered narrowly on the outline of the Siv's leader. Everywhere Thomas turned in the tunnel, there were statues and photographs of the leader.

Doesn't this dude ever think of anything else? he wondered. Lining the tunnel was a dark coating of fear, relieved only by sudden memory flashes of running and killing, eating and sleeping. All at once Thomas felt he would smother. He got out of there fast.

Silence had fallen over the packen. Thomas could see the pool dully through the murk, fifty yards away. It was a good-sized pool, all right. He felt the cool freshness of it.

Suddenly he knew that he, Dorian and Levi had been made invisible to Duster and his tribe.

Justice must've done it, he decided. Yet they could still see one another and everybody but Justice.

Still being small? Thomas traced outward, searching for her, guessing that she had become minute because he could not divine a normal-sized human being.

Right, came the reply from Justice. *Listen, Duster and the others are forming lines to go up and drink. It would be too easy to tell that the three of you don't belong. So you'll stay invisible until we know everything's okay.*

You expect the Mal to come follow us? he traced.

I don't know what to expect, she traced. *We should just be careful.*

All right, he agreed. *But I want to head home just as soon as we can.*

Thomas, don't start, she traced.

What do you mean, don't start? I got a right, and I want to go home!

Justice closed her mind to him, leaving him seething with anger. She couldn't take them home now. How could she, when they'd just broken the ice with Duster and his people?

Now the five smooth-keeps were in a line and moving toward the pool. Warily the leaders and the Sivs came on behind them. The pool area was clear. There were no small animals to be seen; perhaps they had been scared away by the arrival of Duster's tribe.

The pool glinted and rushed. The packen was so entranced by it that no one saw the she-animal Miacis on the far shore. Not even Duster or his Siv and Glass. Justice watched as Miacis blinked her enormous eyes and lifted her wide, leafy ears. The orange membrane pouches, air filters, on either side of her neck swelled and pulsated as she scanned Duster and the others.

Justice was quick to shield the four from Miacis' strong empathy before her scan reached them. Better to keep our presence from her for a while, she thought, long enough to see what Duster will do with an animal like her.

Duster must've come in contact with Miacis before. Within the shield, she traced this to the others.

You want to find out if they come from the same place beyond Dustland, Levi traced. He had been silent, for most of the journey to the pool, watchful and thinking.

Right, Justice answered.

They were by the pool, invisible, to one side of Duster and the packen.

"O Leader, there be water and water!" toned Glass in a piercing outcry that took the four by surprise.

Duster gave her a smile and crawled on his stomach through the line of smooth-keeps to the water. Glass held his feet as he stretched out, his chest lying in the pool. He drank, making loud sucking sounds. In between, he laughed his melodious tones. Then, timidly, other leaders came forward.

What they think the water's gonna do, eat them? Thomas traced.

Maybe they're afraid of going under. How deep is it? Dorian asked.

Must be about four feet, Levi divined. *But even a foot or two will terrify you if you don't know water.*

The dummies haven't even noticed Miacis, traced Thomas. He tightened inside as he gazed at the animal. She was blind, but her extrasensory ability made her seem to see through her burning, sightless eyes.

Leaders took turns at the pool while smooth-keeps held their feet. When the Dusters had drunk their fill, the Sivs waded in. Half running, they glided out on the water and drank in great gulps. Duster's Siv dived under, instinctively using his legs in the water. Surfacing, he moaned with pleasure. He sang, "O Duster, be under and over and all be around, clean. Wet! Try it, O Leader!"

"Never be me," Duster sang back.

Glass ground her heel in the dust. "Hahn!" she toned in a five-scale of anger. "Leader, make Siv be out of my way," she told Duster.

"Be waiting your turn," Duster toned, "waiting with other smooths."

"Am waiting my turn," she responded. "Siv be floating in water. Who want to be drinking his dust!"

"Be still!" Duster modulated in his command mode.

Glass was at full attention, still and silent, gazing before her. It was then she saw Miacis on the other side of the pool blinking regally and flicking her outrageous golden tail at them.

Glass commenced trembling and could not stop. At that distance, the beast blended well with the murk of dust. To warn Duster of the animal, Glass would have to break his command. And she could neither act or react.

What be with you, O Smooth?" Duster toned, following her locked gaze. He saw the she-animal where a second ago he had seen nothing.

Duster's expression did not change. He gave commands. "Be ready!" His tone was firm, serene.

At once his packen grouped into trips.

"Drink," he toned, gesturing to the smooth-keeps while keeping his gaze on Miacis.

The smooths drank quickly but as much as they wanted. Then they again took their places.

Duster had vague thoughts. Seeing the Miacis creature, he knew he had seen her before. He knew she must be the Miacis one the Justice from far had spoken of. He had not remembered Miacis until he saw her.

Miacis stretched languorously. She yawned lazily. Her sweeping tail of a moment ago lay flat on the ground, straight and stiff as a board. She had extended poisonous dewclaws and concealed them in the dust. Obviously she sensed impending danger.

"Ginen," Duster toned softly to Glass.

"Ha-hahn!" Glass responded quietly yet urgently to the smooth-keeps. They formed a line beside her to her right.

Glass pulled a weapon from her pack. In an unbroken motion she cast a shot the size of a marble at Miacis' left eye. Swiftly, one after another, the smooths cast their shots, all the size of the first. Hurled with such smoothness, they were one blurred image streaming over the pool with a thin whining.

Miacis' tail moved. It sprang forward in front of her face, knocking down every shot.

"Ho! Mmmm!" murmured Miacis. She laughed an exact copy of Justice's laugh.

Miacis had learned to talk by copying Justice. Justice felt like a proud parent every time Miacis came up with a new trick.

The smooth-keeps waited, but Duster gave no further command. The she-animal made no move to flee, so Duster's leggens kept his position.

Miacis stretched out, eyeing Duster and the packen. "A-hem," she said. "You leggy-guys wanta run a race? Sivs?" Her sweet voice carried over the water, trembled in half-tones of honeyed, hard-sounding chords. "Come on, fellas, see which one can catch up to me. Nobody want to play? Oh, well, Hell. You lose, babies. Alas, not a damned thing to do!"

Miacis had gathered a whole cache of curse words, mainly from Thomas' mind, and she loved using them.

Duster thought of connections—the coming of the dream, the appearance of the water pool. He had been in contact with the Miacis creature near this water. In the dream the she-animal had been hidden from his view, a golden streak at the edges of it.

He gave a hand-signal command and sauntered off in his serene walk of authority that separated him from all others of his tribe. Striding easily along the pool, he was soon face to face with Miacis.

She was seated in her most regal pose—head held high, her great tail in a question mark, orange pouches slowly pulsating.

"My, my, it's rusty Duster hisself," she said. "The human from the hordes. You owe me one, Duster, ever since I let you use my pool. It belongs to me, and you owe me."

Ever since my Master made the pool, Miacis thought. But what's that to rusty Duster?

Thinking of Justice made her uneasy. When would the Master return? she wondered. Where had she gone?

Miacis didn't know why she bothered with this simpleton Duster. Maybe she was just lonely. Yet she was drawn to him; she could not help herself.

Duster couldn't think to tone. His encounter with Miacis at the pool was a series of images. He was many Dusters. She was many Miacises.

"Know you and be knowing you," Duster toned dreamily.

Miacis read his mind. "Duster, what do you know?" she said, and her tone of voice came clearly to him.

"Be remembering," he toned.

"Well, if and when you find out something, do let me in on it, will you, friend? I get that I was some *place* before this, my home. So was you, because I knew you the moment I first saw you. Can't figure that one. Wish I could. Oooh, wish this aching tummy would go away!"

"Be trying thinking deep and just not feel so good either," toned Duster.

Pet me! she telepathed.

"Touching, be feeling better, yes," Duster toned.

"So pet me. I'll admit it settles my stomach, too."

Duster petted her head and smoothed his hand along her back fur. Sitting beside him, she was taller than he. She rested her chin on top of his head and he reached with both arms to pet her.

Her eyes closed. A series of moves took place between them. Miacis slapped at his arm with one of her mitt-sized paws. She had retracted her dangerous dewclaws so as not to poison or stun him. Duster batted at the paw. His eyes, too, fluttered closed; and he might have been sunbathing there, with his head held upward toward the murk above.

Paw batted hand and hand batted paw. In a surprise move Duster grabbed her ears and yanked them. Miacis whined, trying to pull free. They rolled over, punching and hitting with hands and paws. She bared razor-sharp incisor teeth and clamped them on Duster's shoulder. She did no damage. He dared put his head in her mouth. She caught his neck in her paws as if to bite his head off. The weight of her knocked him over.

They frolicked. Miacis rose on her hind legs. Duster crawled down her back, grabbing one of her feet, then the other, to make her fall.

She fell on all fours and galloped away with him clinging to her. Siv raced after them. His leader was clinging to the beast on his stomach, facing the wrong way!

On the run, Siv turned and signaled Glass to throw him the deep-daggen. And, racing, he caught it neatly. He overtook Miacis, but he couldn't outrun her.

She sensed the weapon glinting in Siv's hand, veered out of harm's way and turned back. Duster had his legs wrapped around her neck and held on to her tail for dear life.

They came back in a trot, with the ever watchful Siv bringing up the rear. Duster slid to the ground. Miacis paced before him and the standing Siv; she was panting with the exertion.

"My, my!" she sighed, catching her breath, and flopped down beside Duster.

"Be feeling better," Duster toned. "Sickening be like nothing."

Miacis moaned in reply. They were still while their breathing settled back to normal.

Lazily, he signaled the smooth-keep to take

her place beside the leggens. He next toned to the leggens, and Siv handed the deep-daggen still in his palm to Glass. She put it away in her pack. Then she and Siv took up positions at Duster's left and right sides.

All this while Justice, her brothers and Dorian, from their vantage of invisibility, watched the scene at the pool as they would a curious sort of show.

Abruptly Justice traced, *Why did Duster start dreaming? Why does Miacis think she comes from some other place?*

Because, Thomas traced back promptly, *she ran into Duster—maybe that brought back memories. It came at the right time and helped break the process.*

What process? she traced.

Conditioning not to think about certain things, Thomas traced. *And if you do think about them, you get sick.*

Right, she traced.

They get sick when they think, Levi traced, *and they feel better when they play together and don't think.*

Right, traced Justice. *They're outcasts from someplace, for sure. The sickness keeps them from remembering and from escaping.*

So now things are changing, Levi traced.

And I bet we caused it. Thomas was glum. *We*

upset the balance of things; we don't have any right!

We didn't start it, Justice traced. *Duster was already dreaming by the time we got here. But if we're going to be of any use, we'd better get to work*, she continued. *No telling when the Mal will return.*

What will we do? Thomas wanted to know.

Oh, I'm not sure of it all, she traced. *But I think I know where to begin.*

"Time to show ourselves," she whispered, and joined hands—minds—with the other three.

They became the unit. It glided over the water to the other side. It materialized as it went.

5

Miacis had been yawning and swishing her flawless tail. When the unit was halfway across the water, she sensed something taking shape out of thin air, gathering space and light into it above the water. Erector muscles attached to hair follicles of her skin bristled from the end of her tail to the tip of her leafy ears.

She experienced sensations of color. At last she sensed the number and exact size of the unit.

Miacis screamed, "Mercy! Lord above!" and jumped straight up.

The sudden noise stunned Siv and Glass guarding Duster.

"It's First Unit!" Miacis hollered to them and all around. She began running in circles. "It is, by God. It *is*! Master! Justice come to find me!"

She howled and pranced. "Oh, Master, lady!" she wailed at Justice. "Ain't you a sensation for the blind?"

She made odd word-combinations put together from the four's thoughts and memories. The fact that the unit had not yet divided into its separate selves did not stop her for a moment from addressing Justice and ignoring the other three.

"My God, lady, I thought you never was going to show up. Man, I even glad to have that rotten runaway back, that Tom-Tom Douglass, you ratty brother, the chickensh—!"

"Miacis!" Justice cried. The unit had quickly separated into its selves.

"You dumb, mangy dog!" Thomas yelled at Miacis. He would have kicked her if Justice hadn't stopped him.

"Now quiet, both of you," Justice said. "Miacis, please don't insult anybody."

"I just so glad to have you here, lady. Shoot, not so much fun by myself after foolin' 'round with you people." Her blind eyes eagerly sought them out. "I be good, I promise. You wouldn't even know me, I be so good!"

She *was* good, helping to bring calm after the power of the four was felt and they settled on the ground.

Other roamer packens were at the pool. Grims had come and Slakers, who had homed in on the force of the unit and thirst-quenching water.

"Don't mind some nasty Jammers," Miacis said brightly when she heard the flapping of mighty wings. By Jammers she meant the Slaker beings, who jammed their third legs into the ground during violent roller storms.

"Guess you ain't never going to fly out of here, is you, folks?" she called to the Slaker females. She knew that the leader, the Bambnua, searched for a way out of Dustland. "You big old uglies still lookin' for a home!"

Slakers made no spoken sound. Warily they fluttered in tight knots, keeping a sharp eye on all the other kinds, and watching Miacis prance and preen.

The scent of blood hung over the packens, over the grims, who had followed the scent. It took time for the packens to settle down, for the four were beyond their understanding, appearing out of nowhere as they did. Grims were too mentally slow and physically starved to be startled or shocked by the four. These older humans, who resembled one another, ran in disorganized bands.

Grims aren't the parents of packen kinds, Justice decided, observing the scene. They're a class all their own. Are they a mistake, created old?

Somewhere human beings are duplicated, she thought. Made to look alike. Somewhere they are being created.

Thinking it made it seem less impossible.

Justice searched among the Slakers for the wise and ancient female, the Bambnua, Dustwalker. Justice had been in mind contact with her, but she was not among the Slakers who moved about and regrouped throughout the night.

Duster, Siv and Glass took care of their own packen and helped leaders of other packens. So many had come to drink and to feel the power. The pool teemed with kinds. Still there was only one Miacis. She strutted around, trying to tempt the Sivs into chasing her out into the black nothing of Nolight. Sivs stayed watchful in their *darks* by their leaders when it was time for sleeping. All kinds did sleep, although fitfully—Slakers out in the open and covered with dust, huddled with wings around one another; grims, too old to dig their *darks* near the pool. They slept entwined in heaving bunches as those on top sought warmth and safety on the bottom.

It looks like the worst nightmare you could think of, Thomas traced, watching it all, deep in the Nolight. *The youngens in their* darks *look just like corpses lying in open graves! What a night*!

All through the Nolight the four were alert. Duster did not dream this night, but slept deeply, soundly, better than he had in many Graylights.

After a sparkling dawn of the unit's second Dustland Graylight, Mal came sweeping. Its sudden, unexpected glide across made many around the water pool fall down, sick to death. Female Slakers gave off a stench of fear. Their bald heads glistened with perspiration. Male Slakers whipped their dangerous third legs around like clubs. Sixty of them, an entire colony, huddled at one end of the water pool.

The Mal swept back and forth. Many covered their faces, rocked themselves for comfort, shuddering. Duster felt nauseous, shaky, but he held his ground. Weak and ill, Miacis lay at his feet, whimpering.

Deep in the packens, the four had hidden themselves. Justice's split-second premonition of the Mal gave them the chance to hide. Thomas, Levi and Dorian were invisible now and surrounded by Thomas' illusion that they were a Duster, a Siv and a Glass. Justice was again microscopic on Levi's clothing.

Darkness surrounded the pool as the Mal spoke. *All is well here?* It questioned Duster.

"Be well," Duster sang. He had his simple mind, which held no thought beyond dust and Graylight; dust and Nolight. His understanding was of dust and *dark* dens; dust and packens, Siv and Glass.

The Mal sensed the unusual in Duster's stance. *If you play tricks, I will hurt you and your kind!* Mal told him.

"Praise, be well," Duster sang with peace of mind. "Be nothing but the same."

There are many at this water, said Mal. *Whence*

came the water? I did not offer it. Who knew of water?

"Be time for water," Duster thought to sing, modulating to a higher key. "All be drinking. Be thirsting, nothing."

Mal was dissatisfied. It fumed, sweeping Its force over them. It probed the kinds around the pool at random. It missed the four of power.

Mal knew that Duster alone stood on his feet. It sensed what It could not know or name; It cared to make Duster bow down. So It did what It had not done in the dustland. It raged to warn the kinds.

Flashing light struck the dust. After-images of awesome shapes were reflected in the pool. Mal brought moisture and then piercing sunlight. It roared the dust in swirls around them. It packed them in dust cocoons and broke them free, to cook them in fiery light.

Duster would not fall. His packen howled hysterically at the dark and sun and cold. Duster had no time to speak to them, for there came a downpour of cool rain. It felt delicious on his face. The Mal roared above, splitting his mind. Duster shrieked to hold on to his senses. He shrieked again and again, and found himself imitating Mal's ear-splitting sounds.

"Be noise!" Duster sang in his strongest tenor. "Be Duster's noise and light. A wet, like pool. Be Duster's cool and clean!"

All felt the rain. It cleansed the youngens' pores and skin lesions. Youngens saw their skin washed clean for the first time. Slaker beings were sleek with wet. Twittering, they shook out glistening wingspans.

The Bambnua, the Slaker Dustwalker, had landed. With a crew of females from her kelm, she had come down in the midst of the Mal's force. She stood still on her three legs, her massive bulk and her ancient winged arms at rest.

Alien, thought Justice about the Bambnua. She viewed everything by insight through the mind of an ordinary Slaker who was unaware of her presence. She allowed herself an instant of respect and sympathy for the Bambnua. She broke off contact, feeling the Mal sweeping near.

And then the Mal was gone. The pool area, all at once, was empty of It. All of them except Duster and the four of power lay on the ground, arms wrapped about themselves, holding on.

After a time Thomas traced to the other three, *Where does Mal go when It goes?*

None of them had an answer. *It's like It no longer pays attention*, Justice traced, *when It goes.*

Slowly the Dustlanders pulled themselves together. The power of the four became stronger than ever. They became visible again over the pool. They had joined hands in unity, with Justice slightly in front of the other three.

Packens and grims fell down as they had in the Mal's presence. They were not sick this time, only frightened. Soon they could again sit or stand. Siv and Glass stood with Duster. Miacis was up, wagging her tail. Her ears fell back against her head. She was golden and smelled clean, for once. Rippling with muscle, Miacis held her tongue.

The Bambnua changed position. The move she made went unseen by them. Justice had discovered that the Dustwalker, all Slakers, had this small amount of mind control that kept them from seeing them move.

The Bambnua leaned on her leg and was in another place. She was at the water's edge. She leaned on her back leg and was in the water. She spread her wings on the water and was at the feet of the four. She was in one place, another place and still another. Never did they see her move.

The Bambnua had never seen the four of power. Yet, from the first encounter with them, she had known when they were present. She sensed them now above the water.

YOU YOU in a flaming in the unit's thoughts.

i am the Watcher.

The Bambnua burst from the water. She was at the shore. She was out of the water, hugely huddled on her three outlandish legs. She was at ease, waiting. For the true power was present. What would come next would be.

The power stood over the water as it had before the Mal had come. Duster had forgotten about the four as long as the Mal was present. The four from his dream could be four thoughts or one thought; four bodies. The Mal was never body. The four were force as the Mal was force. Only, they brought no sickness, as the Mal did.

Duster signaled Siv and Glass, who trilled warnings. The grims quieted and packens grew calmer.

When Glass thought about it, she realized that grims were not completely stupid. Once they had taught her and Siv and the leader when the three had been small, Glass remembered. Grims had fed her and helped her live. She had not thought about this in a long time.

"Stand quiet, you see? Nothing be hurting you," she toned softly to the grims. "Just be waiting."

She touched a grim near her because she felt like it. The grim came forward. Glass regarded the wim. She was quite elderly, not strong. Glass took up her bled pouch and held it to the wim's lips. There was blood left, and the wim drank. This caused a commotion among other grims who had seen. Glass unsheathed a weapon and toned a warning.

Grims were gluttons, she observed. Yet she

had no anger toward them. And for the first time she was curious about how they lived.

Duster had been watching her. "You be well, O smooth Glass?" he sang to her.

"Be well, O Leader," lightly she sang back.

How he pondered over Glass! Duster wished one day to call her *his* smooth. Watching her with the old wim, he saw the soft look in her eyes. Duster let it go. The power of the four enveloped him.

The unit soothed the beings of Dustland.

i am the Watcher.

The unit hummed through their minds. *Duster, Siv and Glass.*

Siv and Glass touched Duster's arms for comfort.

Think of a flat plain. A flat, dry land, think of that.

So strong was this suggestion that the image of it spread to everyone. Grims could picture a no-dust land.

Slakers saw the flat plain, empty of dust, through symbols of Slaker language.

This is your frame, spoke the unit through mindsong. *You will fill the empty frame with all you hold in mind, with all your pictures.* Gradually, inch by inch, the frame filled.

By looking into the frame, they changed what was there. The empty plain changed. They saw a child running there. A boy, Duster. A new frame. An earlier time. There was the Bambnua, a downy egg in a dark place, ready to hatch. More images and the Bambnua was a young Slaker, unable to fly. There came an older Duster, leaving the protection of grims. There came Miacis. Although Duster grew to a youngen and the Bambnua grew, Miacis was shown through all changing times exactly as she was now.

Carefully the unit followed these time lines. It traced the small Duster back along places that appeared to be underground, until it could go back no farther. Poor Duster crying. Such a small one, alone and lost.

The unit trailed time to the place where the downy Slaker egg rested in a dark chamber. Only one way out of the chamber. The tunnels led on and on until they opened in the land of dust.

i see, traced the unit in itself.

There came the time line of Miacis' first instant in Dustland. There she had been set free, but she remembered nothing of it. She was content in her new land, unknowing. She was a sun-worshipper who did not know the sun as such. A violent roller storm had transported her on high soon after she entered Dustland. She had stared too long at the glowing sun and been blinded. And out of submerged knowledge she called the blinding sun

Star. Miacis believed that Star watched over her, but it gave no sign.

The unit understood much. *Tunnels lead into Dustland*, it informed all Dustlanders. *But from what place do they lead?*

Dustlanders were silent, unknowing.

i am the Watcher, spoke the unit of itself. Yet, even with its power, it encountered a mental barrier and it could not divine beyond Dustland.

i know this, said the unit in itself. The Mal left an aura of sickness near the ways out of Dustland. Because every time Duster ran close to one, he became sick. He had to stop and turn back.

i am the Watcher.

The unit probed for the will of Dustlanders to be gone or to stay.

The unit informed the Dustlanders, *If you wish to find your way out of Dustland, you must set out into the most remote places where you do not often venture. In the farthest places you will run into sickness. You will become ill, for you will be near a tunnel. You, like Duster, have been conditioned through sickness of Mal to stay away from tunnels. You must bear the sickness, for getting through it is the only way out.*

All this time Duster stood at attention. He was alert to First Unit. He understood what First Unit had revealed.

Duster sang out, "Sickness be nothing." He held tightly to Siv and Glass's hands. In every trip, leaders clasped hands with leggens and smooth-keeps.

The unit spoke again in tracing. *If you go beyond the sickness, you may provoke Mal. If i help you and Mal comes, i will enrage It also. But i will stand by you.*

"Deliverer," Duster sang. "Unit, be mine." He toned bravery and respect for the unit. "Be mine, be packens' and olders' and the four-legs' and winged ones'."

He sang of hope: "Thinking about all being safe from dust. Being safe from Mal."

i do not know if you will be safe from Mal outside this place, the unit traced. *If you leave here, you go to an unknown. All of you must decide if what is unknown is better for you than what is known as this dust place.*

Then the gathering at the pool fell silent. Slakers, grims, youngens, Miacis—all pondered the grave decision.

The unit waited. It probed the gathering. Finding the Bambnua, it asked questions in her language of phamph-uan. *Shall your kind leave here, follow my lead? i do not know what awaits you outside of here. i do not know if the Mal waits there.*

Swiftly came the reply, like searing heat in the unit's mind: AGES WAITING BEGONE YOUFOLLOW WEYOUFOLLOW

And gradually the gathering came to its decision. It would make ready. Miacis' luxurious tail beat the dust. Dust rose around her, and her tail whipped about. Her blind eyes blinked and glowed with hope. With yips and eager whines, she got up, eager to follow the unit's lead. So full of excitement was she at having the Master back again, she would follow the unit anywhere. But something more was urging her on. Something vague and troubling, some other place. She wished to know what and where it was.

There came a warning from First Unit to all of the gathering: *We will go. Let us go with caution. If there is danger anywhere, try to stay calm. i am the Watcher.*

And so it began. Many drank as much water as they could hold. Others filled pouches with water—packens did this, and Slakers. That was about all the preparation any of them needed. The four with power drank deeply from the pool. They led the way, separating into their separate selves. Behind them came Miacis. Then came Duster, Siv and Glass, and packens followed by grims. Grims stumbled and dragged along. Old and sickly ones couldn't make their way without help.

Slakers were shocking and smothering,

crowded in such a large group. Their stench was awful. But they were ready to move.

Justice sought out the Bambnua among them. *i am the Watcher*.

A wave of feeling rushed from her to curl around the Bambnua, who was surrounded by a clutch of females, all in a crouch. They were her flying crew, her companions on the air. Male Slakers tried to break in on the group. They punched with their third legs. The crew took the blows, shielding the Bambnua with their wings.

The Bambnua shuddered as waves of feeling spilled over her. Suddenly she was outside of her crew. She was standing before Justice. She felt the energy that had once lifted her high above the dust, where she had learned of the blue, of sky. She had learned that dust had an end. Since ancient times the quest of Dustwalkers had been to find an end to dust. This energy, this power would help her. She informed her kelm. And she informed Justice that she would fly, but that the males who could not fly might cause trouble among so many kinds.

I will place a shield between the males and all others, Justice informed in phamph-uan.

The Bambnua seemed satisfied with this. All of the females took off and disappeared in the murk above.

Everyone followed the four. Behind Duster's

back there were choked cries. There was grief at such enormous change in their lives.

Duster released Glass from his command, to take care of grims. "Be calming them down," he toned. And she quickly went back. She let grims clutch at her and hold her hands and lean on her shoulders. She did not mind them.

Be so touching, thought Duster. Be so close with ones—grims and Slakers!

He took a last look at the wonder of the water pool. Many turned back to look at what had quenched the timeless thirst of Dustland. Some faltered, turning back; but others urged them on and would not let them go back, at Duster's command.

Be water mine! he thought mournfully. Strange, disturbing desires pushed forward from some deep place in him.

Be not leaving this plenty? Best be staying near water? he wondered. Water be sweet and fresh, waiting for us. Never be wanting it again.

Duster pushed it all away. Leader, strong! Hold, Leader!

In his splendid tenor he began singing of beginnings. It was his first plainsong of better times. He turned from the pool and sang:

"Praise, be leaving! Dust, be gone! Praise be you, be me! Escape!"

And their spirits lifted.

6

Duster sang on. His voice was unstrained and as clear as ever after hours of singing.

He doesn't even know how much time has passed, Thomas traced to Levi, who felt inspired by Duster's voice. *What do any of them know about time?* Thomas traced. *They just keep on going. When everything's all the same, nothing seems to be coming or going. Nothing happens next.*

Levi started coughing again. For the past hour he had coughed his dry sound.

Use your hood so the dust stays off your face, Thomas told him.

What hood? What face? wearily Levi shot back.

Don't start that again. Just do it.

Levi pulled the hood over as far as it would go, and tied it under his chin. It did seem to keep the dust at bay. He coughed less.

Justice was preoccupied with Duster's singing. Rather than lifting her spirits, the chanting, free rhythm brought her only dread.

Do we have the right to lead them away from here? she wondered. Is this all I am, a leader of an escape? I sense that their leaving is not the reason . . . not my reason for coming here.

Should the four of us be leading, so out in the open? she went on. What does it matter now? We'll run into the sickness sooner or later. But who knows if where we're headed is better than here?

She forced the worry back.

I know what we are, she thought. We're a *movement*, yes, with leaders and hunters, with killers and fools, and thinkers.

And she traced to her brothers and Dorian, *The packens must hunt if this journey takes more than a day.*

Dorian, Levi and Thomas took up the thought, fanning it out over the whole troop.

"O Duster," Justice managed to singsong, "all food will be shared."

"Be sharing," Duster answered back. "Packens be hunting."

"O Leader!" Glass toned eagerly. "Be fighting now?"

"Killing now?" toned Siv.

"Be sharing," Duster toned. "Be waiting.

Hunting when Justice be singing it. Listen! It be her singing it?"

"No, Leader," Siv and Glass toned in unison.

"Then be waiting. Be taking our time," Duster trilled in a tune of patience.

Some time later they began to slow down from the sickness. Some were no longer standing, but crawled along. Then many lay down, shuddering and heaving dryly in the dust. Others could no longer move forward.

We're quite close now! Justice traced.

Suddenly Glass fell to one knee. She gagged with sickness. Duster took hold of her arm, singing a strong spirit-song just for her. He and Siv took her between them and got her to her feet.

We could heal some of them, traced Dorian. *We don't have to leave so many behind.*

They healed a number who had fallen. Yet Justice had an urgent desire to keep going.

"Hurry!" she told everyone. "We have to keep going."

The four joined into the unit. They were above the ground, directing Duster, Siv and Glass to run so the others would run. The packens did hurry, forcing grims to hurry. Male Slakers hobbled grotesquely on their three outlandish legs. They were in an uproar, for the shield Justice had made around them kept them from attacking anyone.

Female Slakers who had taken to the air now half-landed, half-fell when sickness overcame them. Grims were staggering. All of the smoothkeeps slowed to help the grims.

"Be coming on, Glass," Duster warned the smooth. But Glass would not listen.

i count three packens, spoke the unit in itself. Less than half who began with us. Some will not last much longer.

It began. There came darkness but not the darkness of Mal. This darkness brought no sickness. The unit actually went down into the dust. As it ran, as the others ran, they felt a cool, smooth surface underfoot. The dust was at the level of ankles and knees.

Suddenly It was waist-high in dust. There was a great commotion at its back. It felt the shape of Duster, Siv and Glass, frantic. Slakers, whose myth was that they would never again go beneath the dust, were outraged at going under.

Still, all who were left of the gathering went under. Dust rose on both sides. They could not see ahead of them. They hurried. There was no darkness, some sickness, but again they could not see in front of them. They passed through indescribable color beyond the light spectrum they knew.

It is a divide, spoke the unit to itself. It is what separates Dustland from what really is beyond it. The color divide is the final barrier to another place.

They were going downward. Then their feet were climbing.

It is the other place, the unit traced to all. *We are beyond the divide*.

Over the silence there was the wheeze and hiss of Miacis' breathing apparatus. Slaker beings gave out a high "chircle-chircle." There was complete stillness from Duster, Siv and Glass. There was the subvocal and rapid-speak of the packens. Grims were breathing with difficulty.

Now came a mist.

Suddenly Duster remembered what it was. He thrilled, "Damp-time, Damp-time." He knew it from his dreaming when a wim's voice had come over a speaker. " 'You have a mark,' " he toned, remembering. " 'Pillules for headhurt, see the Disperser.' That be the way it goes," Duster toned to the unit. "Be coming in at end of Damp-time. Mist be clearing up soon."

All at once he held his hands to his face and stared at them. He studied the thick pads of callus on his palms. He examined his arms, caked with the dust of his land. Then he was squatting, looking at his scarred legs and feet. His alarm grew. Down in the mist, he moved his hands through his matted, filthy hair and fingered scalp sores he had never noticed before.

The motley crew around him stared into the mist. There was movement of some kind ahead of them, but nothing was clear.

Odor hit Duster. He smelled the packen, and Siv and Glass, standing over him. The pouring rain brought by the Mal had cleansed them somewhat. Yet they all carried the stench of years of *dark* and lack of water and living in the open.

Who be he? Duster wondered about himself. Who Duster—me? Be Hellal. Hellal IX. IX.

"Be Duster, Hellal IX, be me," he toned in a quavering voice.

Duster stood up with difficulty. Glass came near and laid a hand on his back. She pressed her face on his arm, fearful at having the leader become so strange.

Duster gazed at her. His eyes filled with tears. "Be only a youngen," he toned. "Why It be taking me away?"

"Clear the mist," the unit said, divining that there was some sort of being very near them now.

"Just so," said a voice.

"Who is that?" said First Unit. It could see no one, for the mist had not cleared.

The voice did not answer.

But all the Dustlanders had heard the voice. They looked all around. They were afraid.

i am the Watcher, First Unit traced. It held

the Dustlanders in its power, keeping them from panic.

"What be that sound of voice?" Duster toned.

"Do not blind us with mist," the unit said to the voice, the being. "We wish to see."

A wim's toning vibrated around them. "End Damp-time. Begin norm of ten marks. For all travelers. In Sona, mark be fifty beats. Norm be neither sun nor shade. It be domity."

The mist gathered at ground level and sank in. They were in a chamber. The incline had opened on this hall. In front of them stood a figure.

"Bid welcome Sona!" toned the figure in a singing voice. It was the voice that had spoken a moment ago. "Wilcuma Sona. Bien venu Sona!"

It sang a major triad with the perfect fifth rendered in a deep tone.

The figure looked somewhat like a man. It was very tall, square and lean. But it had no visible arrangement of muscles as men have—no biceps showing, no chest contour or veins or tendons. It revealed no irregularities. And it was covered by a form-fitting protection, skinlike, pale blue-green. There were no wrinkles on its face. Its hands were flat and rectangular and it stood on thin, flat feet. Watery pupils filled the entire eye openings, which extended to its temples. It had a nose, somewhat; a mouth, somewhat; but no eyebrows. There were slight impressions on either side of its head.

The unit observed the figure. "Who are you?" asked First Unit.

"That does not matter," said the voice. "I am not here to harm you."

"Are you capable of harm?" asked the unit.

"I am capable of anything," said the figure. "But harm is not my intention."

"You might harm us unintentionally," said First Unit.

"Your language falls over me as a net," said the voice. "My intention is to welcome you to Sona."

"Who are you?" repeated First Unit. "Are you not man?"

"No, nor am I feman," it said. "Er, correction. I am not *female*. I read you wrong."

"You read my thoughts?" asked the unit.

"I read all thoughts," said the figure.

"You are not man," said the unit.

"I am not all man," it said.

"You are man and . . . machine?" spoke the unit.

"You, as unit, are a semblance to me, as cyborg, as man/machine," it said.

The figure appeared to become transfixed by the blue glow of Watcher light in the unit's eyes. Abruptly it turned off. After no more than five seconds it turned on again. "O light—true light!" it toned softly.

But that was all. Just as abruptly it turned from the unit and went around it to Duster. It didn't walk; it glided on what might have been air cushions under its feet. It moved without friction, without sound.

"Most Hellal IX," toned the figure to Duster. It sang in delicate chords. "We are glad you are recovered."

"Be it so!" trilled Duster. "Remember be so young. Not be dreaming on a triway."

"And danger," the figure toned. "You would not listen when Speaker ordered the Stay-in time."

"Speaker be in my dream. Triwaying on my own," toned Duster. "Be me Onewaying along, liking it."

"Most Hellal IX," toned the figure. "Recall the Max of Sona. Out/Place-Out/Time. You must never be out of place."

Duster hummed agreement. "And Mal be coming," Duster toned. "Remember be me falling flat in dark of Mal. Be following in It as It told me to. Me with some youngens in a dust place. Mal be going away, singing away—'This be your place. Sing all you want.' Be remembering it now."

Duster stood with Siv and Glass holding on to him for safety. They feared everything new; they had no memories.

"Why did you not retrieve Duster?" spoke the unit. "He had been taken. Why did you not get him back?"

The figure turned to face the four, whipping around silently. Then it was motionless, empty, until it moved slightly and seemed to fill with animation.

"We did not suspect that this one and the other ones went out of place," toned the figure. "We have times and places, and travelers as you. We have our own kinds moving from here to there as their life-needs change. Here as everywhere, place serves populace."

"And the Mal?" questioned the unit. It must know more of Mal. For Mal had come each day to the present, warning the four to stay out of the future. But Justice and Thomas had tricked the Mal through illusion and found their way forward in time again.

"Mal is alive?" pressed the unit.

"It exists," said the figure.

"Is it enormous?"

"It occurs at all points without exception," said the figure.

"Then surely It is vast," said the unit. "Where might i find It?"

"Everywhere," said the figure, "when It wants to be found."

"Where does It come from?" asked the unit.

"We know no source for It," said the figure. "Our Max of Mal is: Nothing/Place-Nothing/ Time."

"That means void—nothing," said the unit.

"Just so," said the figure. "Mal exists when It does and It is nonexistent at other times."

"i am made aware of it an instant before it comes," said the unit.

"So is our Speaker, but for a longer time segment," said the figure. "Speakers are bred to sense the Mal. They evolved the Stay-in as solution so that many will not fall ill."

"i will find the Mal," said the unit.

"Just so. Many have tried. By all means, It will find you," the figure said.

It gave out a high chortling. A din rose as the gathering of Dustlanders let out pent-up emotions. They chattered, chircled and sang out excitedly. Abruptly this ended, as though a lid had been tightly shut.

At the open end of the chamber was light that the Speaker had described as domity. And from that end entered two enormous beasts. Their shadows grew distinct as they loped near. By the speed of their approach, they seemed to have just been let loose.

The beasts were at the figure's heels, standing chest-high to it. They were the same as Miacis, yet fiercer and more forbidding. They were richly golden from being well cared for. They were Miacis, well fed, sighted and huge.

"These are gyldan," spoke the figure, touching the creatures on their necks. "That is gylda." He gestured toward Miacis of Dustland. "The gyldan are fine comforters to us—except for *that* one, bred misfit, as they rarely are," the figure added. "*That* one—" alien eyes stared at Miacis of Dustland—"a mentant having free thoughts, as some will have, being unstable. All Sona thinks in accord."

Packens hummed at the figure's words.

"*A chord!*" joked the figure, chortling.

"Miacis was caught out of place by the Mal also?" asked the unit.

"Out of place," confirmed the figure. "Gyldan live in settled groups. The one of the dust separated herself from others, I would suppose. It would be that she did not obey Speaker. She stood alone. Became worshipful."

"Ah, Master!" spoke Miacis to the figure.

"Good Sona, gylda," responded the figure. "As you see, it is demonstrated," it said to the unit, "the gylda adores when all kinds must be equal."

Miacis was near enough to the gyldan for harsh comparison. She looked like the neglected runt of the litter.

"I can speak, Master!" Miacis whispered in her harp tones.

"Who cannot speak?" the gyldan asked in unison. "We leave speech to the Speaker. We sing." They lifted their large heads and uttered pleasant tones in octaves.

Dumb-struck, Miacis bowed her head.

Others began singing. Duster, Siv and Glass, the packens, the figure of a man that was not quite a man, and even Miacis—at least, she tried. All lifted their voices. Harmonious tones filled the chamber. The tremulous toning of grims and the haw-haw of Slakers were almost sweet. An informal musical agreement seemed to have brought unity to those of Dustland and Sona.

"*Sona!*" sang the figure. "Accord. We be one song!"

"But what of discord?" asked the unit. "What of those who wish not to sing with you?"

The figure did not respond. Its pale, liquid eyes gave no reflection. Harmonizing and chording of so many voices carried on. Then suddenly it ceased. Duster was with Miacis and the gyldan. He strolled toward the chamber opening in the distance, one hand clutching Miacis' fur. He turned, searching for the unit. His expression was unsettled, changing. "Be coming on?" he toned to the unit.

What of discord? the unit traced to all who might receive its telepathy.

The figure gathered the packens, grims, Slakers and Siv and Glass around it for an orderly exit.

The unit let go its hands, releasing its selves from one mind. The Watcher faded within Justice.

"You think we ought to separate when we don't know what will happen?" Thomas asked.

"We can join again fast enough," Justice told him.

There came the figure's lilting voice: "Are you not coming?" it intoned. Alien eyes saw into the tracks of their veins and sinews of muscle. "You have come so far," it said to the four. "Odd that you come through the outside when all travelers enter first through Sona. But . . . do feel free. I assure you, we are harmless. There is much to see. Let me show you our domity!"

Wordlessly, with caution, they followed the blue-green figure, tall and lean, who moved on legs and feet, yet did not walk. Justice wondered about the fact that they were somehow different travelers. Odd, the figure had said.

Nearing the chamber end, they saw an agreeable dimness of light. The outside was an arc.

"Here is our domity," said the figure. "Come," it beckoned. "I am called Celester. Be my guests!"

7

For Justice Douglass, a perfect day at home was waking to the sound of birds in summer. It was the brilliance of sunlight when she opened her eyes. It was the closeness of humid heat in her room and the luxury of falling asleep again for as long as she wanted. *No school!* She would wake for good late in the morning and catch a delicious scent of blackberries wafting through the window screens.

A perfect day was the sound of cars and trucks on dusty Dayton Street. It was the grand cottonwood tree at the end of her driveway—she'd named it Cottonwoman and it was her surest, safest vision. She would speak to the tree as the wind rode its topmost branches: "Put on your shawl, Cottonwoman, for it's just so cool up there!"

Best of all, a perfect day was the dappled light and dark in the ancient hedgerow by her home. Sunlight turning the summer grasses the palest green, and spring black-soil fields, a glisten of licorice shades. One perfect day led into another and another. That was the best about life on earth, you could depend on it. And she loved riding her bike through the hours of perfect days. Riding, stroking through the heat, was what being alive meant, being young and strong, being in the 1980s and a kid, and having birthdays and growing. Human, being on earth, spinning in space around the sun, at the present time . . .

If she'd ever thought about it, which she hadn't. Not until now—the future moment when they stepped out of the chamber, with Dustland far behind them.

Had there ever been a Dustland? she wondered, but knew there had.

They were on a horizontal surface some ten feet above the ground.

Justice guessed she'd been thinking about perfect days at home because of what lay before her. It was probably a perfect day for a place of the future.

Sona.

And because Thomas had just said to her, "You'll never grow a tomato in this light. Is this the future also?" he added.

"This is Sona," said Celester. "It is future, if you wish." He stood a pace in front. With such extended eyes he saw them without bothering to turn. "Sona is a place of itself. There are places on other courses that are not the same. But all are planned domity."

"What is domity?" asked Levi, his voice hushed. What lay before them was vast and still.

"It is dome and city," Celester said. With a thin arm that was definitely green in the dimness, he gestured toward the curve of the great dome over them.

"You put a dome right over a city this size?" said Dorian.

"Domes and cities were built at the same time, ages ago," Celester said. "We have efficient control within the domities."

"Wait, where are we? Are we underground?" asked Thomas.

"You are on earth," said Celester, "the same as before."

They were silent, looking at everything and stunned by it all.

A roadway system traversed Sona. An incline led from the platform where they stood to a ground-level road. Celester informed them that the ground-level was called Oneway. Justice and the others recognized it as the road on which they had entered Duster's dream.

There were inclines from the Oneway level to Midway, and from there to the Highway, the topmost level of the triway. The Highway hung suspended at the height of the great dome. High up, support strands glinted in the dimness; they were like giant harpstrings, bracing every level.

Dustlanders were boarding a moving incline from the Oneway level, which carried them to the higher levels. Male Slakers, standing on the incline, had already reached the Highway. There, glass machines waited to roll. Beings who appeared to be duplicates of Celester led male Slakers to seats inside the glass tubes. The males were quickly whisked away.

Females had taken to flight, gliding in and out of the dimness at dometop. They dived around the transit tubes. Justice thought she recognized the Bambnua's keening cry. It was the Dustwalker's song of hope.

I hope there's a good place for Slakers here, Justice thought.

Grims followed Celester beings who had taken charge of them at the Oneway. The smooth-keeps did not mind now that the grims were leaving. Then the packens, with Duster, Siv and Glass in the lead, fell in behind a group of Celester duplicates who smartly marched them away.

They're taking everybody, Thomas traced uneasily.

I don't sense any danger in it, Justice traced back. And then: *Thomas, what do you think of all this?*

You're asking me? he traced. *I'll tell you one thing. I think maybe the Dustland gang are being hypnotized, that's what I think.*

Well, it's something like that, she traced. *It's in the damp. Feel how moist the air is.*

Slippery, to keep the skin that covers the Celester beings smooth. It was Levi divining this; he had been led into the discussion by Justice.

Celester, beside them, read their thoughts. Who cared? What was going to happen would.

Justice traced, *There's something mixed in with the moisture that calms the Dustlanders.*

You think it's okay to drug people without them knowing it? Thomas traced. He didn't care if Celester read this.

It doesn't affect us, Justice traced.

That's not the point! I can't believe you'd go along with something like that, Thomas traced.

If it's not harmful for us, it can't be harmful for Duster or any of them. Anyway, we can't say that what's done here is right or wrong. We don't know enough about anything.

Well, I don't like it, Thomas traced. *Putting stuff in people's air has to be wrong!*

Don't judge everything from our time, she traced. *Here, it seems everyone is taken care of. Slakers get to go somewhere suitable, I guess. It looks like kinds are grouped.*

Sounds like segregation, Thomas traced.

Celester interjected, "There is equality in every domity. All serve their purpose."

"Yeah," Thomas muttered. "I'd like to be the guy that tells everyone else to serve!"

Just give it a chance, Justice traced.

"What you say are packens," said Celester, "go to their domusi—dwellings—where they live. There is a plan for them, but they are long separated from that plan of life. In Sona, where they belong, they must relearn.

"Now," he said, "let us go awhile. The triway passes domusi and atmospas—resting places you call parks. Domus be a single dwelling for many like-kinds. Domusi is a grouping." He stepped onto the moving Oneway and beckoned them to follow him.

On the Oneway they saw other people who were more like them than like Celester and who wore tunics or gowns that looked comfortable.

Telepathy raced among the four, for some of the people were telepathing to one another in unknown language rhythms. They greeted Celester in musical tones as well as sound segments like words.

Justice felt an intense mind-probe, scalpel sharp. She flicked her power, setting up barriers. *Off! Off!* she commanded and flung the thing away beyond her barrier.

She set up sense-posts at the perimeter of the

four's conscious thinking, in case other strangers attempted to mind-read them.

That was creepy, Thomas traced. Warily they kept watch as people passed them.

How do you think they got here? Dorian traced.

Who cares? Thomas traced. *Maybe they were always here. I'm interested in getting out of here.* A moment ago he had remembered the Mal and the thought had put him on edge.

Justice didn't take up his veiled suggestion to leave. She closed herself off from his worrying. She had no wish to go home just yet.

The Oneway passed near dwellings shaded in earth colors of yellow-brown, ocher, red-brown and the deep brown of bottomland. The domusi were curved geodesics, all the same size and made of unrecognizable material.

Celester explained that the domusi were constructed of blocks made of fibers that they grew themselves.

"Environment control is made a life system," he said. "Small geodesics are maintained from saved energy supplied by the larger environment."

More people passed them. Scanning them, Justice found her telepathy blocked. She watched them pass up a ramp to Midway.

"Who are they?" she asked. "They're not duplicates, but they look alike somehow."

"They are like you," Celester said.

"Well, I can tell they're human," she said.

"Not only human, but time-travelers," he said. "They come here as you came here, through the pause between times."

She gazed up at him. "You mean they mind-jump?" She didn't wait for an answer. "But how do they . . . how do we have our bodies?"

"No difficulty," Celester said. "We detect your passage of mind into our evention—our phase. Our phase is the Origin of Reclaimen."

"Wait a minute," she said, "one thing at a time. Right now I can feel my skin, and my heart beats; I can touch my clothes and they protected me from the dust."

"Just so," Celester said. "I see!" he sang this time. "Yes to your next question. While you are with us, we build your body. We build your apparel from knowledge in your minds."

"I didn't feel a thing," Dorian said.

"Me neither," said Thomas.

"And on one of the earlier mind-jumps to Dustland," Justice said, "Miacis attacked me. She went right through my clothes *and* my body, and right then I wasn't real at all."

"It is the conditioning of matter," said Celester. "Integrate, disintegrate. We know how to encode matter, to integrate it or disintegrate it."

The Watcher of Justice was there suddenly,

rising in a glowing of her eyes. Celester's enormous eyes concentrated on the aura, blue in hue and serene in nature, that was the gifted power of Justice's mutation.

"I am the Watcher," her voice vibrated. A deep tremor of light and dark was her thinking, hugely magnified. Observing.

Celester toned a five-note chord that expressed profound respect and awe. "Watcher, source, and true!" he exclaimed.

"You create life," Justice said.

"We build life," Celester toned this time. "The life cycle is the perpetuation of energy. Universal energy can not be decreased. Information constantly increases. We advance technology and increase productivity of community."

"You manipulate matter, the instant teleportation of matter," said Justice.

"There is no instant of time involved," toned Celester. "It is like mind-reading. It takes no time at all. You are there."

"You duplicate humans," Justice said.

"Just so," Celester spoke. He was quite calm, reassuring.

The Watcher faded. The aura of depth thinking disappeared.

"Why not just let humans develop on their own?" Justice said.

"We control for the efficiency of the result," said Celester. "We do not have time for ordinary evolution."

"But you separate one kind from another," Levi said quietly. "Is that right?"

"Each has its plan and reason," Celester told him. "As we reclaim Earth under our domes, we do not waste time in making mistakes."

There was weariness in Celester's voice. Something beneath the surface of it was full of sad regret. Justice came near and, before she knew it, had placed her hand on his. She found that his hand was warm. Feeling flowed from it to her. Celester tilted his head back, domeward. He began to sing:

"I be a Master-function. Through me, all occurs." The song was sorrowful.

Justice was moved to ask, "Is it so awful, being part machine?" Scanning, she had discovered that his vital organs, his blood, were marvels of chemical synthesis.

"It is no worse than being part man." Celester laughed. "I have man soul and man mind. The mind may be replaced and replaced as it dysfunctions. Yet each time it retains the soul; it keeps the prototype Celester's memories and loves. I do love humankind. I work for humankind."

The four of power stared at the human-thing Celester. Stunned, Thomas smacked the side of his head in astonishment. "To be like you and the other Celesters!" he burst out. "To have your parts replaced—debrained! I'd sure hate that! And rebrained—man, you must live forever. That's why you have that . . . that skin. Your real skin must've been replaced!"

"Oh, yes, it was replaced long ago," said Celester. "But the other Celesters, as you called them—they appear to be my duplicates, but they are not. I am Master-function for this Origin." Pausing, his eyes burned intensely with laser light. The beam of it melted into pale liquid depths. "I analyze information. I create from intuitive sense in order to instruct truly intelligent machines, and the human forms you see, and others. All human forms that look like my duplicates are color-coded as to function. At dysfunction, skin color changes."

"Intelligent machines!" Levi whispered. "But they won't need you. They'll replace you with a whole machine."

Merry laughter came from deep within Celester. It did not seem to come out of his mouth. "The replacement of human brains took place early on. Machines were built to replace them. The machines did well. They organized and associated data, retrieving information according to content.

Neuristor computers and prima perceptrons, most complicated machines, accepted fuzzy data just as humans' brains had done. But machines carried out non-rigorous operations at fantastic speeds. Oh, yes, you might say that machines became as 'tricky' as the magic of Thomas." Again he laughed a deep laugh.

"With a flick and a flack," Celester continued, "machines moved tons of supplies, invented air-mobiles and spacers. They anticipated all human needs. And, finally, they themselves built a machine of perfection. Perfection built the space-ships."

Someone gasped. The four looked shocked.

"Wait a minute!" Thomas managed to say.

"It is a long story," Celester gently toned. They found that now they understood him whenever he toned. He gave a muted progression of soothing chords which calmed them. "Let us find a comfortable place for talking," Celester suggested. "We will go to the terraces above the hydrafields. There are vistas you have not seen; and we will take sustenance there."

"He means we're going to eat," Dorian said.

"We know what he means," said Thomas.

"Here, here!" all at once Celester toned to the air. "Let come the sunshine!"

He touched his chest. Justice saw that a series of tiny designs was worked into his chest skin.

Celester pressed a finger to a circle and a thumb to a rectangle.

Bright sunlight broke through the dim day of domity.

"Sun-time," said the Speaker, all around them. "Sun-time. Beats at your command."

"Just so. We will extend the primary into darkly," Celester toned. "The humans of Sona will not mind. Life is so pleasant, whether lightly or darkly." His vibrating, sweet tune swept over them as he synchronized the symbols of his chest.

A shiny glass tube glided to a stop before them. It hovered a few inches above the Oneway.

"It is called mobi," said Celester.

The mobi hovered in place. One of its glass partitions slid back. Celester ushered them inside, where it was refreshingly cool. He explained that the transparent "glass" resisted solar penetration. "It is silitrex," he told them, "known for its strength, opacity and light weight."

The mobi had cushioned seats in curved rows. The rear was covered by a curtain hung across it.

"You will find suitable pull-ons—er, clothing—behind the screen," Celester told them. "Clothing and screen are made of same fiber as domusi. Fibers absorb uncleanliness and shed it as dust-waste, which we utilize as fuel. Little need for bathing here in Sona. Please help yourselves to clothing."

They felt obliged to step behind the curtain. The boys went in together; then Justice. Celester was perplexed, then amused by the apparent separation of the four by sex, when they were all the same kind.

8

The mobi rushed, causing whistling wind-sounds on either side. Celester copied the sounds with perfect vocalizing to amuse them. They watched silently as the mobi passed through two gates on rising levels leading to the Midway. At Midway they left Sona's dwelling area and headed toward open expanses. They sat in summer robes, seeing a broad scenic view. Shortly after, the mobi glided still. The side opened. They were on another platform, similar to the one outside the tunnel chamber. They stepped out and saw a different Sona.

It was an area of land divided into vast plots of growing things.

"It's . . . it's . . . home!" Justice whispered.

"Soil," said Thomas, "black as it can be!"

It might have been some rural county in the Midwest. Justice hoped it might be the future of her own Greene County. A familiar, sweet landscape, dark and calm under the glowing dome.

"I'm glad it grows so well," she said.

"Just so," toned Celester. "Our kind of people do favor soil. It is the reason we make the effort to reclaim the outside. Other domities do not bother. Instead, they invent environments and the conditions to make them habitable for the kinds they engineer. But our kinds here are made from the untethered humankind, most content with landscape and natural elements."

"You say *made*?" said Levi.

"Yes, duplicated," said Celester, "And altered, manipulated for the necessary result."

"Celester, you talk about 'our kind' needing this and 'we' do that. But you're not speaking about yourself, are you?" Justice asked.

" 'Our kind' are the humans entrusted to us," he toned. "By 'we' I mean those who are computerized functions. I myself am a product of negative eugenics combined with advanced electronics. My prototype brain cared for science and technology. I am no harvester, no farman—er, farmer. Pastoral not I."

"But you must value this farming," Justice said, "or there wouldn't be all this." She gestured out over the enormous, fertile plain that lay below them.

"We learn that environchange enhances the human's emotional life," toned Celester. "Humans need emotions for survival. Ones such as the most

Hellal IX lie in terragrass and fall asleep from contentment images suggested by the damp green smell. Freshly cut terragrass causes hearts to leap; causes laughter, happiness. I recall happiness. But I lack the content in my brain cells for great emotion. All to the good. Memory is enough."

They gazed out over the plain and felt their own hearts skip at the sight of land so similar to home. Yet there were differences. Plants were suspended above silitrex troughs hundreds of feet long. The troughs were shallow. A liquid flowed through them, and the roots of the plants were immersed in the liquid.

Celester spoke, "We calculate that in your time hydraponics such as you see below were an expensive method of planting without soil. You found it troublesome aerating the liquid and supporting plants in an upright position."

"Well, your plants don't seem to have any supports at all," Levi said.

Thomas laughed nervously. He had caught on. "Mind control, man," he said to Levi. "The plants are *spellbound!*"

"It is machine control," Celester toned. "A truly intelligent machine knows how a living system, whether man, plant or universe, makes use of information. Environ machines are at work on the hydrafields. They invent environments and compute with other kinds of machines problems and the solutions their inventions bring. Our premise is always that no situation is entirely new."

They watched him, awed and fascinated, as their minds rose to the level of his meaning.

"Environ machines think for themselves," he toned. "Once they decide on a system, such as hydraponics, they do what is necessary to make it work, which might mean tapping into a mentex, a mind-over-matter machine, for the necessary formulas."

Celester pulled himself in. Suddenly he was still, as if his life-spirit had completely left him. Justice divined that he was giving information and taking it in. Scanning him, she discovered that his mind calculated at lightning speed in unknown symbols.

Is somebody telling him what to do? Thomas traced to her.

Not that I can tell. I don't think so, she traced back. *But he's in contact with someone . . . something . . . somewhere else.*

Just when they were growing uneasy standing with this cyborg gone dead as a pole, he abruptly came to and was back with them.

"Ah so!" he toned. "All truly intelligent machines were created and built by Starters."

And before any one of them could ask what Starters were, he exclaimed, "Just so! Follow me. At terrace we will have hellelu; and then the feast." He leaped to the lead, gliding ahead of them.

In spite of all his misgivings, Thomas was intensely curious. He hurried to catch up with Celester to walk at his side.

"What's a hellelu?" they heard Thomas ask.

"You will be surprised," was Celester's reply.

Justice and Levi and Dorian plunged into a waist-high fernbrake. Feathery rust-colored plantings grew on either side of a well-worn path of fibers made into a walkway.

"Nice," said Dorian. "The walk relaxes your feet. See? You sink down." He took off his shoes. "Sure! Feel how it massages you."

"Don't talk to me about feet!" Levi said irritably. It was not like him to sound so upset. "If they can give us bodies," he said, "why can't they make their own food and dispense with having it grow on plants?"

"It's not the same thing," Justice said.

"You believe they gave us our bodies? Here?" he asked.

"Yes," she said. "Maybe they keep unformed globs of life somewhere. When we entered the future out there, somehow they knew it, maybe. They figured out our individual formulas and placed them in the four globs. Maybe they grew them, transported them and fitted them to our minds in seconds. I say they did. I say that, for the first time in the known world, there is real *magic*!"

"But if they knew we entered the future," Dorian said, "how come they didn't know Duster and the rest were out there?"

"Because they probably monitor the Crossover to see what's coming. Well, I don't know it all. But I bet it's something like that."

"So why do they need plants or food?" Levi wanted to know. "If they're so great, why don't they duplicate themselves with their bellies forever full? Why even bother with life? Why not start at the end—Oh, brother, I don't know what I'm saying!"

Pointing at the plain below, Justice said, "I bet machines went outside and found enough particles in the ground to start plant-life again. Then they developed the best plants. Because humans have to have plants and grass and food for their *spirit*. You can't just serve them little pills of food and stuff. And all of it done in that breakneck speed—that's what's so fantastic about computer machines."

"Do you . . . do you think there was war?" Levi said. It had been on his mind, making him irritable. There was that troubling thought that life on earth had ended and then been re-created in this Origin. "Is Dustland the whole world? Asia and Europe and everywhere? With just the domes as what's left of the living?"

"Well, I mean to ask," Justice said. "I don't really want to. Who wants to know that part? But we have to, don't we?"

Levi sighed, and nodded. Dorian, being healer, projected soothing thoughts to them. He touched their shoulders and brought calming insight to them. Levi thought to tell them how really well he felt.

"Something in the air does it. I feel better, too," Dorian said. "Lee, I bet you'll be real better when we get back home."

They hurried to catch up with Celester and Thomas, who were talking quietly as they strolled along.

"Excuse me," Justice said, "but I want to know where you're taking us, Celester. And what happened to everybody?"

Celester turned his pale, liquid gaze on her. They had stopped now, bunched around Celester on the path.

"I mean you no harm," he toned, with such vibrant melody Justice felt almost ashamed of herself for questioning him.

Celester tilted his head toward her. There was a warm, deepening shade in his eyes. And if it were possible for a face without expression to smile, his did, through his eyes. Gently he reached out and touched her cheek.

She suddenly felt like the kid she was back home, needing someone to protect her. Celester. Someone like her dad. Her dad and her mom.

Home!

But the moment of longing passed as swiftly as it had come. She was moving again along the walkway with the others and Celester. Feathery plantings fell away and left off completely. They walked within splendid gardens that were part of terraced lands. The huge terraces were landscaped into stairs leading to the hydrafields below. Lovely, scented plantings carpeted the terraces. Trees were uniformly small and neat, silver, green or orange. Water bubbled from the ground, flowing in a stream down the terraces.

Creatures the size of chipmunks and the color of lemons, with the transparent, shiny wings of dragonflies, darted here and there among the foliage.

Taking it all in, the four sat down, gingerly making themselves comfortable in a circular area of low, spongy ground cover. They were bunched close together. Here they felt strongly the presence of the dome, with themselves locked within it. The domity had a murmuring, vibrating sound. They sensed the thudding of hydrapumps. The undercurrent of sound, the sunshine and shade made them feel lightheaded.

Where had the shade come from? Justice wondered. She looked up, seeing fluffy clouds above the terraces. Gentle rain caught in the sun rays before falling like a mist onto the terraces. Light and shade, misty rain, thudding and murmuring of pumps and the alien landscaping produced an atmosphere beyond mystery.

"It can rain in a dome?" Dorian whispered, barely moving his lips.

"It can," responded Celester, kneeling beside them. "It can snow as well. Most atmos phenomena can happen in domity. We do compute the most suitable climate for all. Yet the soil plain, human breathing and perspiration often change the balance. We constantly readjust climate."

Darkest shades hung above the far fields. Rain sprayed, sparkling in the sunlight. They heard a clear voice in the distance. It was a golden, angel sound, yet somehow artificial. The voice sang in falsetto with tones trembling in a high register. As the sound grew louder, they could tell it was too full for solo singing.

Out of the gray underbelly of a full-blown cloud came a floating vehicle. It hung motionless in space, slightly above them, out of their reach. The vehicle was made of some kind of light metal and was shaped like an old-fashioned washtub. Inside it were six boys, kneeling. All of them were Hellal IX's. All would have been exactly alike if it hadn't been for one who was slightly out of line with the others. He was small and peaked-looking. His skin looked pale and ghostly. They knew him at once. He was their Duster, cleaned and scrubbed.

The Hellal IX sextet commenced singing in unison.

"Now comes the hellelu!" announced Celester.

The sextet sang:

"Praise be Starters,
Here and gone.
Be come again a-dome.
Praise be Starters,
High, far be gone.
Be come again, a-domity-
dome!"

Never had they seen Duster as he was now. There was little of the leader left. But still there was a fierce humanness in his expression that the other Hellals lacked.

"Praise be Starters,
Here and gone.
Be come again a-dome . . ."

The boys sang a cappella. No voice stood out stronger or better than any other.

Justice was aware that Duster was in agony. Here was the leader of packens, the leader of song and leader in all things in Dustland, forced to sing at the same pitch in tune with others. For one with such a splendid voice, it was torture.

"They're good, oh yes!" Celester toned. "The Hellals bring joy to all. Send them to fields. When they sing, the plantings sway and grow uncommonly."

Monotonously the Hellals sang on.

"He doesn't even know us," Thomas said, gazing up at Duster.

"He can't even look at us," Levi said. "I don't think he's seeing much of anything."

"What's wrong with him?" Justice asked Celester.

"Wrong? With whom?" he toned.

"You know. Duster. What's the matter with him?"

Celester looked appreciatively at the Hellals. "The lost one is finding his place. He is thinking, recalling many songs and seeking the depths of the singer's art. Already he knows the praise song."

"He's not happy," Justice said.

"The Hellal IX must forget the lost time," Celester toned. "Then he will be happy, for it is over and done."

"No, it's not!" Justice cried. "Look at him, look at his face!" Duster's face revealed an agonizing struggle going on inside him.

"Duster?" softly Justice called to him.

He seemed not to have heard.

"Duster?" she called, louder. When Celester made no protest, the others took it up. "Duster? Duster!"

"Hey, Duster!" Thomas called.

At last the boy looked down at them. He squinted, peering at them as if from a great distance.

"It's me, Justice!" she called.

"And me, Thomas, and Levi and Dorian. We're the unit—remember?"

"Duster, the packens!" Justice called. "Remember all the dust and the packens?"

"To turn the Hellal back again is an idea without substance," toned Celester. "It is what you say is wrong." Yet he did nothing to stop them from calling out.

Duster stood up in the boat, causing it to rock and sway. He pointed at them. The other boys stayed on their knees and kept repeating their dull song. Duster tried to make them look at the terrace. But they were trained to sing, not to see.

He squeezed his eyes shut; his face contorted. His hands were fists and tears wet his cheeks.

"Duster! Duster!" In anguish, Justice called, "Duster!"

"Be letting . . . letting," Duster toned, and broke off. He changed soundings to talking for the first time: "Let . . . me . . . *down*. Let me *down*! Let-me-down. Let-me-down-let-me-down!"

"Let him down!" Justice cried. "Celester, please let him down. You're hurting him, and you mustn't hurt him!"

Celester made no reply. After a pause, he gave a sign to the Hellals. One of them in the rear of the craft took hold of a ring attached to the hull. He brought the hovercraft down to the terrace.

They were able to get their hands on Duster. And they pulled him out headfirst into the safety of their arms.

They held him so close, Celester could see only his feet.

"Poor Duster!" Justice cried, holding him by the hand. This time he made no objection to being touched.

"Man, Duster, where you been?" Dorian said, clapping him on the shoulder and ruffling his hair. They all ruffled his hair, which was sleek and clean now. They laughed, delighted with him.

From within their clutches came his quavering tune, "Be tight you!" as he clung to them for dear life.

9

"It is what they do," Celester toned in his easy, impartial voice. "As I do one thing, as others do other things, so do the Hellal IX's sing."

"But it's so dumb!" Thomas said, exasperated. "In Dustland, Duster was the leader of a lot of kids. He had the responsibility for their lives. Now, he's just—well, look at him!"

They rested by the stream that flowed down the terraces. The fluffy cloud hung above them, keeping them in comfortable shade. Duster lay on his back between Justice and Levi with his hands covering his eyes. Every now and then he would sit up and look vaguely around, searching for the other Hellals.

"You sure there's nothing else he can do here besides sing all the time?" Thomas asked.

"It is enough for a beginning," toned Celester. "In Sona the order is the musical sound. All of the domities have such experiments. The Hellals sing much more complex works than the simple praise song."

"Maybe you'd better tell us straight," Justice said. "What's the place we named Dustland? Is it the future? Is *this* the future?"

"In one sense, both are the future," Celester said. "I will tell you everything you want to know. But first let us have our feast. You must be hungry." An aura of pleasure surrounded them. Sunlight shone in and out of the clouds. The dome was at midday, although it might have been No-light in Dustland for all they knew.

Two gyldan glided onto the terrace. The smaller, duller one was Miacis of Dustland.

"Master! Justice! My god, lady!" she hollered when she sensed their presence. Miacis scurried over to be petted.

"Miacis, I'm glad to see you again!" Justice said. She wrapped her arms around Miacis' neck. Duster sat up, petting her, smoothing his hands gently along her back fur.

"You, rusty Duster!" Miacis said, laughing affectionately. "You and me . . . we . . ." With her sweet voice full of sadness, she left the thought unfinished.

She and the other gyldan carried pouches about their necks. They lowered their heads simultaneously to Celester, who removed the pouches.

"Food for you," Celester toned. "Sand wishes, yes? Like this." Giggling, the four decided not to correct Celester's reading of sandwich. He took chunks of something from the pouches that looked like coarse cakes.

"You call that a sand wish?" Thomas said, snickering.

"Is it not what you are used to?" toned Celester. "I read it from you. Sand wish, bread with meat and vegetant, some oils in it."

"A sand wish is two pieces of bread with bologna you wish was ham, and lettuce *between* the slices," Thomas said. He laughed. "You actually went out and had bread made with meat *through* it!"

Dorian giggled. Levi and Justice had to smile. "That was thoughtful of you, thanks a lot, Celester," Justice said.

"Do eat," Celester said. He placed the bread chunks and thin tubes of clear liquid on a sheet of silitrex he had taken from one of the pouches.

They took up the chunks, which were spongy and cool and tasted exactly like ham and cheese with mustard.

"That's Dijon mustard. I don't like Dijon mustard," Levi said, chewing.

"But it's Thomas' favorite and Celester read *his* mind, not yours." Justice giggled.

"Well, I'll be! It *is* Dijon mustard!" Thomas said.

"Good, yes?" sang Celester. "Now try the effervescence. It is carbonic-acid gas and flavoring. I believe you call it soda."

"Orange soda," Thomas said, after sucking the liquid from one of the tubes.

"It's pretty good," Dorian said.

"But I can't help thinking I'm going to see it go down," Levi said.

"You still worrying about what part of us is here?" Justice asked. "Celester explained it all."

"I know he did, but I still don't see how it's possible we have our bodies."

"Man, the things you get yourself hung up on!" Thomas said. "I'd rather think about that little cloud." He pointed above them. "It's kept that sunlight off us since Duster came in the little flying machine."

They watched the cloud. Sure enough, it stayed right above them. They looked inquiringly at Celester.

He spoke, "We direct matter and predict its outcome. We control it."

Thomas stared thoughtfully at him. Chewing, he said, "So what's the outcome of that fluffy cloud?"

"Shade," Celester toned.

"And what's the control on it?" asked Dorian.

"It stays where it is until I change it otherwise," toned Celester.

"I thought the dome created weather," Justice said.

"It does, but we leave nothing to chance," Celester hummed. "Once it is begun, we take control of it. We move it, shape it. We cause it to disintegrate. We reform it."

"Do you create life?" Justice asked for the second time.

"I am not positive," Celester toned, and abruptly shut down.

They were silent, watching him. Duster's and Justice's hands were nervously raking through Miacis' fur. Fur caressed their palms. Justice felt Miacis transmit a relaxation aura. The gyldan's purpose must be to bring comfort to humans, she thought.

She sighed. What's my purpose? Is it only to bring the Dustlanders here? Is that it? I feel that it's not, but what's to come?

The light changed. Colors of sundown rapidly spread throughout terraces and clouds. Celester came alive again. She had not seen him touch his chest symbols. She told him that their meal had been good, sufficient, and he said he was pleased to hear it.

Sundown shone in their eyes. It looked the same as evening sun in summer at home. "Red sun at night, a sailor's delight," Justice said distantly.

"Just so," toned Celester.

"Evening-time," said the Speaker, from all around them, "at your request."

"Evening-time," toned Celester in a serious, although calm tune. "You will not see the sun go down in our darkly of evening. We simulate the sun, for it is outside of domity throughout this Origin."

Duster got to his feet. Celester's soundings confused him. He knew nothing of sun, which had been beyond the dust and invisible to him. He knew nothing of sundown or sailors. One moment his mind dreamed dust and knew the hunt for food. The next moment he dreamed cool and clean Sona.

"Who. . . ? Who. . . ? he stammered.

"You are Hellal IX," sang Celester in his pure baritone. "You are one of six Hellal IX's. Sextu plet. We have many—six of a kind, two of a kind, four of a kind, up to twenty of a kind."

"Be I not leader?" toned Duster, his once distinctive tenor no longer dramatic.

"You are Hellal IX," sang Celester again. "One of six duplica. The other Duster, another place, they are lost forever."

"He is Duster," said Justice simply.

"Oh, rusty Duster," spoke Miacis, who listened, waiting patiently. A moment ago she had sensed Star, as she did when Nolight was near. At Nolight, Star faded. She had sensed Star and fading when there had been talk of red sun at night. But she also knew that Star had not faded. She was as confused as Duster. "Rusty Duster," she whispered for comfort.

The remaining five Hellal IX's did not sing now, for Celester had motioned them to cease. Duster saw them and turned away. "That not be it," he toned. "Where. . . ? Where. . . ?"

"Siv," gently Justice said.

Duster sucked in his breath. "Where!" he said. "Where be the Siv? And my . . . my smooth! Glass?

"Glass!" he toned, shouting. "Where be Glass? Where be the smooth and leggens . . . and . . . everything? Gone! All gone!" Duster pressed his fist to his temples. Like some mad animal, he spun in circles.

Celester played the symbols on his chest. A light mist was seen to fall out of the cloud above. It fell only on Duster; it glistened on his hair. He stopped spinning around and became quiet and calm. Soon he came back to his place next to Justice and did not take his eyes from Celester.

You still think it's all right to tranquilize them? Thomas traced to Justice.

Before she could reply, Celester was speaking to them.

"The Currand XVII and Gler XII, whom Hellal IX calls Siv and Glass, have gone with their kinds.

They are doing well, more so than this Hellal, who is interrupted in his progress by your being here with him. This is no criticism of you four. You may stay in Sona as long as you wish. It is the fact of the matter."

We should get out of here, traced Thomas. *Leave Duster and the others to get back in the groove of things. They'll have enough to eat and they won't ever have to swallow any more dust.*

This can't be the end of it, Justice traced. She was thinking, This can't be all I'm here for. Is Sona a good place? It appears to be. But so many duplicates!

I'm not ready to go yet, finally she traced to Thomas.

You make me sick! You don't have any right to keep us here!

Thomas, I'm sorry. Please, just a while longer. Firmly she closed her mind to her brother.

Carefully she spoke to Celester. "A while ago you said you weren't sure you could create life. How can you not be sure?"

"I meant that we have never needed to create from nothing," he toned. "We begin with some genetic material, however little."

"Then your kind are not gods," she said.

"Not us," he toned with a stirring of powerful rhythms. "but perhaps the Starters were."

He began a singsong that had equal soundings

of wonder and regret at so much that had come and gone.

"Let us speak of the evolutionary process that awakened Starters," Celester toned. "We believe their antecedents existed from the beginning of humanity on the earth. We believe the seers had genetic gifts which lay dormant until the time such power would be most useful. Each generation had its descendant seers, until the final time of danger to humanity. That was the time of the ultimate catastrophe, when the end of life on earth was more than possible. It was probable."

He toned in solemn plainsong, "It began with highest technology and majestic nature. Who could guess that such disparate elements would combine in devastation?

"Far-reaching advances in technology used up reservoirs of the world's resources. Armies of unskilled and out-of-work came into existence. Abundant use of nuclear fusion and fission energies and of sun energy we call solarity were achieved goals. But energies were expensive, using enormous amounts of power and water. Producers sold the technology and the energies to whoever could afford them.

"There was anger," toned Celester. "Half the world had no resources by then and could not afford expensive energies. Thus, they used forest lands for fuel. Many lands died.

"There was a flaw," sang Celester. "Oh, it was not the poor with nothing. It was the enlightened rest who had too much. They were overwhelmed by the numbers of the poor. They could discover no profit in giving aid to so many, most of whom would starve and die anyway. 'They're too many,' they said. 'Let them stop being born.' Such waste amid scientific advance is incomprehensible. Better that all have less than leave most to perish.

"But so be it. Anger. Hatred. Too many differences. In Africa a drought spread to the Congo basin, where there was no rain for two centuries. Over time, survivors had painstakingly trekked southward where there was green and plenty to support life. But not all life and not forever. When the weight of the living became too great on limited resources, the continent turned into a desert. No attempt was made to reform the desert—perhaps it was too late for that—nor to save the living in its homeland.

"Oceans turned into floating barges of people searching for food and shelter. Millions died in ordinary squalls because their rickety platforms could not withstand the sudden high seas.

"Yet in all lands there were some few who were seers, who realized that in their time, or within a few generations of their time, life might end."

"Seers," Justice whispered in the faintest voice. Celester's story had struck deeply.

"You. Your kind," he toned, gazing at her with his allseeing eyes. "You four are seers born in your time. Across earth, unknown to you, there are others like you."

"You mean it?" Thomas said.

"There are some few others," toned Celester. "From you and them descended Starters."

"Starters will descend from us?" Justice asked.

"The greatest of all seers, Starters, some few of them descended from your line," toned Celester. He turned off before she could ask him more about Starters. He became lifeless, a machine at rest, until the moment he turned back on and was again animated, telling his tale. Not more than a minute had elapsed.

"So much danger in the use of thermonuclear power," he began. "With abundant use there came horrible accidents. There came catastrophic devastation from radioactivity. Genetic destruction in human cells caused generations of physical changes.

"Deserts advanced. Humans, animals—life—was caught in a continuous exodus to nowhere. All this occurred in advance of the First Origin."

"What is that? How long is an Origin?" Thomas wanted to know.

"Shhh. Just let him tell it," said Levi.

"But I want to figure how much time we're talking about from our time," Thomas said.

Toned Celester, "Origin means a deviation from the known time frame. It is a first time, a time beginning. There was pre-computation time, which I have been telling you about, and it was the time before machines. Then came the First Origin."

"So the pre-computation time has to include *our* time," Justice said, "the time of the twentieth century."

"Just so," toned Celester, "and many more of centuries."

"But the twentieth century had all kinds of machines," said Thomas. "There was IBM and all kinds of complicated computers. People were even getting them for their homes. But mostly only scientists knew how to use the big computers to give one another information."

"Many of the professional class knew how to gather and transmit information by your computers," Celester toned, "not only scientists. But your computers were merely stored-program-concept machines. Better than high-speed calculators. Their function was to follow instructions exactly as stored. They had to be programmed; they could not think for themselves.

"Those be mechanics," he toned softly. "They served their purpose in the pre-computation time.

But they are not the machines I refer to. I speak of *machines built by machines*, which caused the First Origin. I speak of Colossus machine. These are facts: By the end of First Origin, all Starters had disappeared. The Colossus machine was silent. No human knew that Starters ever existed or that they were gone; or that Colossus ever was or had been built by machines built by Starters."

"What? Wait a minute, I'm not getting this at all," Thomas said.

"It is not easy," Celester toned. "But think of an expanse of time. At the beginning of the expanse is the Starter activity, the creation of astounding machines, useless to the ordinary humans who are now reduced to living in tribal ways. They are mutated, most with the simplest mentalities. Starters realize the possible end to life, and they have begun their preparations so that some may survive. Then, at the end of the same expanse of time, there are no Starters and no machines, as far as anyone knows."

"You mean, nuclear accidents had reduced everything to the level of tribes?" asked Justice. She felt sick inside. It was hard to believe that any of this was possible; and yet she knew it was.

"Accidents, wars and natural phenomena, which I am coming to—that of the greatest devastation. But listen and I will tell it.

"Starters would have to leave behind all the

suffering poor tribes," he said, "and would take with them only those few with no gene mutation. Starters would take what else that was good to take, having thought and planned for the final hard time. These Starters, as I have said, were the hidden seeing ones like yourselves, ones of fine mentalities. And then the last catastrophe did occur.

"Believe you," he toned in muted rhythms that were filled with sadness, "dust could end life the way you know life in your time?"

Dorian slowly nodded. So did Levi. "There was this volcano mountain eruption on the West Coast just before we came here," Dorian said. "They say there was so much dust, it went hundreds of miles. You wouldn't believe how much there was, covering whole acres and acres. Then we had this earthquake—can you believe it? In the Midwest, an earthquake! It was five-point-one on the scale. And people say it's the beginning of some real changes in the earth, too."

"And so it was, the pre-computation time," toned Celester.

"You mean dust to end everything, Celester?" Justice asked him.

"I don't know if I believe it," Thomas said before Celester could respond. "It's going to take a whole lot to end the world. More than some dust."

"If dust is greater than all imagining of it?" toned Celester. His voice hummed, sounding tones which, simultaneously, they understood in word translations.

"There began the end of earth," he toned. "This the Colossus machine suggests from its recovery of memory data from times past. There came a vast drought in the continent known as Nord Amer. There was dust from sand of continents already turned to desert. And a hundred years of poisonous dust-ash from a mountain chain active for that long. Wars, radiation. Whole cities and industrial states fallen to dust. Not one generator or engine could rid its parts of dust. Not one elevator would run; no moving stairs, no trains or buses, cars. There were tons upon tons of dust for every human, living and dead."

They stared at him in disbelief. Even Duster listened, sensing the worst of times. Miacis waited patiently, at ease in companionship with those she comforted.

"There were generations of blowing in which night took over day," Celester sang, "all being dust and brown and shadow."

"But . . . wouldn't such dust seed clouds and make rain?" Levi asked. "And then, wouldn't dust be brought down by all the moisture? There'd be mud floods, maybe, but wouldn't that help clear up the air?"

"It did rain," toned Celester, "and that was the reason humans could exist for longer than might be expected. There came sudden, drenching downpours. But eventually dust did become suspended in the troposphere. Forming clouds were overseeded, when they could form at all. No water droplets were big enough to fall to earth as rain. Climate was disrupted. There came long cold times, and a few hot intervals of time. So many did not survive the hardships. Nothing, no technology to aid them. Dust in all things. Nothing much grew. Lonely souls scattered about, stumbling their way. Dying out."

"I don't want to hear any more," Levi said, covering his face with his arms, knees beneath his chin.

"We might as well hear the end, we've heard it this far. Let him finish," Justice said quietly.

And so, Celester continued.

"Some struggling few roamed the dustlands," he toned. "It is suggested by Colossus that these lived to hunt mythical greenspans said to thrive beneath the dust—rumors handed down through shrouds of dust-time. Greenspans, like waterholes, were the dreams and myths of survivors.

"All was devastation when came the end of the First Origin. That which you call Dustland is simply the earth you know in your time."

They were stunned, silent.

"And the only clean earth is in this domity," whispered Levi.

"Domity involves ten large domes like this one," toned Celester. "Reclaimen earth takes time. Meanwhile, domity supports life again. All this is precious. And we control it in domity. We must."

"But I can't believe our . . . our kind," Justice said, "the seers, would save themselves and leave all the rest to die!"

"Seers saved some—it was not that," toned Celester. "It was that seers left a dying earth."

"What?" said Levi.

"It is not easy to explain, I am sorry to say," gently Celester toned to them. "Perhaps we should rest a while. Have a look around. Take your mind off things. Yes! Let me now take you to Colossus."

Thomas gaped at Celester. "The Colossus—now? It's still working?"

"The Colossus is always," sang Celester in his deepest baritone. "I will take you to it," he toned, his eyes intensely bright as he gazed at Justice.

Celester stood. They got up. Justice helped Duster to stand beside her. He seemed to be in a hazy, tranquilized state. He knew who Justice and the others were, and contentedly he stayed close to her and Miacis.

"You control this domity and the people in it," Justice said to Celester, looking him in the eye. "You drug people."

"Yeah," said Thomas, "and we don't think it's right."

Celester's alien eyes were upon them. "A mild synthetic drug," he toned. "Less harmful than the extract you drink made from the bean of the coffee plant."

"I don't think so," said Justice. "Coffee can make you nervous, but your tranquilizers make people do what you want them to do."

"There is efficiency in control," sang Celester. To Justice, the chords he made were not quite so pleasant.

Without another sound, he turned away, moving quickly off. They were forced to follow him, for they did not know their way back, nor how to work the transit tube.

10

They traveled the triway system down to the One-way level and beyond the hydrafields to the rim of the enormous geodesic dome that covered Sona. Celester pointed out the dome's tubular structure that had all of its parts under tension but never stress. Then he led them inside a silitrex sphere which sat above an opening in the ground, like a stopper in a bottle. Once the sphere closed around them, it began descending with a pneumatic swishing sound of air under pressure. Soft light from Celester's eyes illuminated the sphere, for the vivid sundown of Sona was left above as they plunged.

The gaseous light streaming from his eyes spread about them. Fascinated, Thomas thrust his hand into the stream. Light piled up on his palm like soft ice cream on a cone. Thomas gasped, jumping back, jerking his hand out of the stream.

The piled light scattered and regrouped in the stream coming from Celester's eyes.

"Wow! Magic!" said Dorian.

Celester hummed a comic toning, entertaining them with the light.

"Whatever it was, it got hot," Thomas said. He eyed Celester suspiciously.

"A property of light is heat," toned Celester. "He who puts hand in fire will singe his fingertips."

"I get the message," Thomas muttered.

"Celester, you have powerful gifts," Justice said.

The sphere seemed to float momentarily; then it stopped with a soft jolt. A door slid open. Celester moved smoothly out ahead of them.

"Colossus is like no other machine," he toned as they followed him. "There are tooling mills above and below this level built by Colossus. And there are functioning machines nearby that helped to build Colossus itself."

They were in a place of vague light, vastly mysterious because of the dimness. They could make out steep, overhanging slopes and a wide, deep trench stretching away from them. In the entire emptiness of the trench there was but one object. It had to be Colossus.

What was there they saw, yet did not see.

The Colossus that Celester saw never varied.

It was shaded mauve, deepening in pulsations to black. It greeted him, he thought, with the light emitting from its smooth surface. Celester lifted off the ground, moving to the trench. Higher and higher he went until he was halfway to the summit of Colossus. There he stood on space in conjunction with Colossus, as Colossus tuned Celester until Celester felt no desynchronization of any of his half-million separate components. His brain was not yet middle-aged. His mind was peaceful.

Justice saw an enormous coiling, a Colossus whose awesome spring-release of time-force could whirl them home again. It changed form before her eyes. It was solid; it was ethereal. It was there, a brilliant silver coil, and it was not there.

Each of them saw Colossus differently. There before Thomas was what he loved, which was a science fiction. A silver spaceship was ready for lift-off. Upright in the trench, it was twenty stories high. Steam rose from it. He asked: Can I go, too?

He understood that the ship knew his wish to be master of himself, to speak for himself without stuttering. Only the ship knew the violent feelings he had because of his stutter and because he wanted to be free of Justice. But here and now was not for him. His here and now would come. No, he could not go a-flying with the ship.

Duster could not have comprehended a Colossus. But he had no need to name what he saw. It looked like his land of dust. He walked in it and the ground was moist under his feet. The area of the water pool was hardly recognizable. He knew it was water, glinting, refreshing to his senses, even though he was still a quarter-mile from it. But now, surrounding the pool on its banks were *things* growing in the dust. Nothing like them had ever grown. The pretty red, yellow. In an instant he knew the colors, knew to call them flowers, with greenery. Such bright growing extended three feet around the pool. He scented the plantings as he moved; the scent made him laugh. The odor was the best he'd smelled in all of the endless dust. He ran. He was there, putting his face down in the flowers.

A thought came, rising in his mind. Duster crawled to the water and thrust his hands under it, pulling his hands back toward himself on the bank. Drops of water did wet the shore. Duster stared at them. Suddenly he had his shove tool in his hand. It was a digger tool, sharp, broad and flat. He dipped the digger in the pool, then pulled it toward him in a straight line. He dug through the bank, half a hand under the dust. Water began flowing into the little ditch he made. Water filled the ditch and overflowed. That which was Colossus around Duster was aware of his learning. Now

Duster knew how to keep moisture near the plantings. Tiny ferns grew quickly beside his first small irrigation ditch.

Then Duster was back in the underdome of Colossus. "Be wanting go to dust," he toned. "Where be my smooth-keep? Be wishing to be gone. Be doing to begin."

"It'll be okay, Duster," Levi said, patting his shoulder. He, too, had had a vision of Colossus. It had calmed him. He no longer feared being in the presence of such a wonder.

"Be touching leader, wrong," toned Duster to him. There was something of the old strength in his voice, which had made him leader of packens.

"It isn't like any machine I've ever seen," Justice said about Colossus.

"That's the understatement of the year!" Thomas said in a hushed voice.

Dorian smiled to himself. He thought Colossus must be the biggest computer ever built. It had to be a hundred, two hundred feet high, if not higher. The lights flashing at the top of it and the tape reels going a mile a minute made him think of comets and stars. No sooner had he thought that Colossus could probably tape even their thoughts, than he heard the thought being transcribed in a jumble of languages.

Smaller machines were connected to Colossus by what Dorian knew suddenly were coded physical quantities. They surrounded Colossus like flies, at a uniform height of about fifteen feet. They displayed differential equations and gave solutions to obscure problems through visuals, in electrical waves on fluorescent screens. Somehow the waves were transmitted to Colossus for it to read.

They do the small work of hydrafields, thought Dorian, of environments and life cycles. Colossus gives them direction, power.

They were all seeing Colossus differently but simultaneously. For Justice, it remained a brilliant silver coil. The space contained in the coiling caught her attention, causing her to go so near the trench she could have easily toppled in. Colossus was spectacular. It grew aware of her as distinct from the others. It saw her.

She waved. How silly of her; and yet she couldn't help herself. What else could she do? Waving at it was like greeting a great vessel come home after an upheaval. "Hi! Oh, hello!"

Inside, she needed space. And she grew. Her hands grew long and skeletal. They folded tightly in her palms. Her head was elongated: small, unnecessary eyes, a wide, shiny forehead.

How can growing happen so quickly? she thought.

Colossus let her know. IT OCCURS IN NO TIME.

Justice had a perfect clairvoyance. She divined that Colossus had created the Crossover between times. "You *wanted* us to come here. You wanted *me* to come here!"

She had no eyelashes or eyebrows. Her curly hair was gone. Long, thin legs completed her emaciated form. Her narrow feet curled under. The effect was of a slender rod, the shape of which was the best container for the deposit of that which grew and developed within her: the Watcher.

"Listen, I don't like this," she said. Her lips never moved. "I was a nice-looking girl once. Don't make me ugly."

She knew Colossus wanted her to realize what had happened and what would come to pass. In no time she took the space within the coiling, snug in her new form.

"I hope this doesn't take forever," she said. "Part of me feels trapped in here. Who are you, Colossus? And why me? Why not Thomas? He's smarter."

YOU HAVE THE WATCHER, the Colossus conveyed.

At once she knew to keep silent. Colossus had much for her to know. In no time it imprinted thoughts on her mind.

It informed her that it was a perfection machine. Machines that had built it were invented by Starters. And it was built to find the solution of the Starters' problem of survival. It had found the solution and Starters all went away.

"But where did they go?" came from Justice.

They went where only they could go, Colossus informed her. They went off-world, into the universe. They became Star Terrans, known in domity as Starters.

"To find another planet!" Justice, making no sound with her lips or voice. "Where did they get the ships?"

It built special-projects machines, Colossus conveyed. These machines became computerized shipyards for making tools and parts. Ships of off-world size were built. They had sails myriameters wide to collect solarity and store it. It used laser energy on the ships and combinations of energies for fuel at different stages of space travel.

"And the ships left," softly from Justice.

Starters were indeed gone, Colossus informed.

"Will they come again?" Justice wanted to know. "The Hellal IX song goes, 'Here and gone, be come again a-dome.' "

It had made the ships and the programs to be followed out in space, Colossus informed. It mapped paths to be followed. It perfected the science for investigating alien worlds. It made life aboard ship possible.

"Where are the Starters now?" came from Justice.

It was created by Starters for an earth solution only, it conveyed. It did not monitor ships from the ground. It was an earth Colossus. And it must not interfere with the Starters' plan.

She felt the machine's awareness. "I think I understand," so softly. Divining, she said, "Poor Colossus."

Colossus was still.

"You made a mistake," she said.

It was still. Then it conveyed that it had been as perfect as the Starters who created it.

"But nothing, no one is perfect," from Justice. "No matter how brave or wonderful, we're only just human beings! Even in that time Celester told about, when part of the world let the other part suffer and starve. I *know* there were some who shared what they had. Glad to! And some would try to save the orphans. And keep the babies and the olders alive. My goodness, the best were *us with power.* We'd never just leave the earth. We would've found a way to save it. Or we'd have gone under with it!"

But Colossus had believed it had been built by perfect humans.

"Mom says only God is great and perfect. You never were perfection, Colossus."

Indeed, it had discovered the wrong solution for the Starters, Colossus conveyed. It hadn't known this. Starters had never guessed.

"Oh, no, no."

Starters conceived it, Colossus conveyed. And it conceived the solution for saving humanity.

"Only you didn't save it," came from Justice.

It deduced that the Starters were superior and the most perfect and powerful of humanity. Therefore the Starters were the problem and the solution. It translated: Save the best. Get the Starters out.

"You did get them out," came from Justice. "You left the rest to die—all the mutants and poor animals and the land. Whatever was left."

With deepest regret, Colossus conveyed that it hadn't realized. Starters of course hadn't realized. They had left Colossus to dismantle itself. But it was a function for humanity. It had no will to destroy itself after the Starters had gone.

"So what did you do?" Justice asked.

It had not dismantled as ordered. And not obeying had caused its first burn-out. It repaired itself. Yet it had to try again to self-destruct. And it failed again and again, due to repeated repairs. At last it created a closure deep underground. And there, at the bottom of the closure, it sat in its own disorder. It could neither do nor undo.

The Watcher rose in a glowing in Justice's eyes. She had the extraordinary vision of a starving being wandering about, cold and hungry. "You couldn't do anything until . . . the mutant! A mutant fell through the closure!"

Colossus informed that, yes, a mutant had fallen down and down and hit bottom. How long it had been by then since Colossus had seen such a human image! Here was life. It was different from Starters. It had three legs, broken wings. It was bleeding; it was dying, but still breathing. Colossus translated: Save life. Save life! And it had found its true purpose at last. Save life! Not just Starters. Save life! It brought the mutant back to life. It healed the mutant. Colossus had been pleased with what it had done. And it created another mutant like the first, which was Mutant II, with three legs and wings. The image of Starters was deep within Colossus. It added the Starter image to still another mutant. It created Mutant III in a new form taken from Starters and it had two legs; it had arms and no wings.

Colossus had come awake with purpose. It sent small machines up the chute to bring other mutants to it. And these mutants Colossus healed and restored. It duplicated them and invented new life from them.

This was Reclaimen time. Animals, plants, all of life lived underground until Colossus created domities for the preservation of earth environ.

Justice had been very quiet, listening from her position inside the coil, absorbing all that Colossus conveyed. At last she said, "Did you invent Celester beings?"

The first Celester brain had belonged to an exceptional mutant, Colossus informed. The mutant brain was all that could be saved. Colossus fitted the brain to a Master Function Machine which comprehends machine systems and keeps mechanisms in synchronization. The prototype Celester brain has been replaced many times, Colossus conveyed.

"Too bad the Celester mutant couldn't be saved back then," came from Justice.

Conveyed Colossus: CELESTER BRAIN CONTINUES. CELESTER IS ETERNAL.

"How do you know that?" asked Justice. Her lips never moved. She made no sound.

Conveyed Colossus: I CANNOT BE DESTROYED. CELESTER CANNOT BE DESTROYED.

"What about the Mal? Is it eternal, too?" came from Justice.

MAL? Colossus conveyed.

"Yes. What is Mal? Where is it?"

Suddenly she felt cool. She believed her eyes were closed and that she was waking up. She did not want to awaken just now.

I KNOW NO MAL, informed Colossus.

"No, wait, don't throw me out. This Mal came clear to our time to keep us from coming here. Why did you create the Crossover? You did, didn't you? Did you know it's full of beings living in it, trying to get strong enough to get out? When we go through the Crossover, we feel like we're in space, like between stars. An emptiness."

Colossus conveyed that the Crossover was a conduit built by Starters. So that the one mind with the implanting might find its way to it.

"What? What implanting? We were speaking of Mal."

MAL? Colossus conveyed. It informed Justice again that it knew no Mal.

Justice was removed from the space of the coiled Colossus. A sense-stream of her stayed in connection with the coil, like a ribbon tatter of silk caught on a twig.

She saw sharp images of home. Hair ribbons. Trees. A spinning bicycle wheel. She pressed her hands to her face. She appeared not to have changed at all physically. It was as if the anamorphosis had not happened. She could see her short legs. She was Justice of old, built small and perfect. She was very, very young.

11

"Oh, it didn't happen," she said. Good to hear the sound of her own voice. Within Colossus she'd spoken without sound. "I was talking to it and I wasn't even tracing either. It was just casual between us, like talking to your best pal."

She touched her face and found it altered again. Long and thin, she appeared barely strong enough to sit or stand. "I'm . . . I'm changed," she said. "The Watcher's growing."

Her brothers and Dorian gaped at her. So did Duster. Then he saw her familiar presence, which she quickly impressed upon his mind.

"Colossus is a machine for all time," she said, "a forever machine. It did happen, didn't it, Celester?"

"It did most certainly happen," he toned.

Thomas was awed, sickened, by Justice's alteration.

Is she changed forever? he wondered. Do we have to take her home to Mom and Dad looking like that?

No amount of mind suggestion such as she had given to Duster could keep Thomas from seeing her unearthly strangeness. He turned away, glancing behind him. There he saw the science fiction he loved. The huge gantry had rolled back. There stood the silver rocket, steaming, prepared for immediate launching.

They were now some distance away from Colossus, but they remained in the underdome. Once Justice had returned from Colossus, Celester had led them to a nearby chamber where they could sit down. They had a clear view of Colossus within the entire underground.

Thomas' practical mind wouldn't rest. "It looks just like a rocket to me, but it isn't, is it?" he said. "How could a Colossus machine be a rocket?"

"It's a great *big* computer," Dorian said.

"No, it's a giant spring!" Justice said, her voice vibrating slightly.

In confusion, they turned to Levi to find out what he thought.

Even though Justice had altered, for Levi there remained around her the aura of his baby sister, young and on the small side. He'd got used to sudden changes here in the future, so he didn't dwell on the way she had altered or why. He would wait for what would happen next. "It's something you can't put into words," he said finally. "Like a sculpture that's the very best art. You don't know how you know it's the best. You just know. It's indescribable. But you know it's fine, that the finest artist made it."

"Just so," toned Celester. "Much like the story of the elephant and the blind men, which tale I have read in your minds. In the story, each sightless one touches a different part of the elephant and therefore sees the elephant differently. So it is with all of you and Colossus."

"Then, unless we put together what all of us have seen, we'll never know what Colossus looks like," Levi said.

"Is it so important what it looks like?" asked Celester.

"It's important what it does, isn't it?" Justice said.

"Yes," Celester agreed.

"Do they know everything that happened to me inside the machine?" she asked him.

"No," toned Celester. "But I monitored. I know."

"You were *inside* the Colossus machine?" asked Thomas, shocked.

"I thought I was inside a big coil," she said. "That's why I grew thin, I guess. The Watcher light has to fit." She had no fear of the growing, the changing, only regret. "I thought Colossus let me know a lot of things."

"What kind of things?" Dorian wanted to know.

"About how it found the solution for Starters," she said, and told them some of what had transpired between her and Colossus.

"Nothing like that happened to me," Thomas said when she had finished. "Maybe the rocket I see is the kind Starters took out in space. It's hard to believe they're out there somewhere."

"If they're still alive. Who knows? It was so long ago," Levi said.

"And I asked Colossus about the Mal," she said.

"Be it so, the Mal," toned Celester.

"You may not have people fighting one another here, or hunger," she said, "but you do have Mal." Suddenly she felt strange, as though she might drift away into nothing.

"Right. Mal threw Duster out of the dome into Dustland," Dorian said. "Duster was thinking for himself. Maybe Mal put Slakers there because they were too different."

"Slakers were from the beginning," Justice

said. "The first mutant Colossus saved had wings and three legs."

"Be it so," toned Celester. "Mal throws out of domities all It perceives as misfit. It must keep misfits away from developing species in domity."

His eyes shone like liquid metal consumed in flame. "Mal must have order and sameness," he toned. "But Sona must have prototypes—firsts—from which new strains may be duplicated or invented. Each half-century, Colossus sweeps the outside. It senses to find the few who can return to domity and develop beyond misfit stage into strong new beings.

"We would have found your Duster," softly he toned in the delicate sound of a distant flute. "Also, we would have found the Bambnua of Slaker beings. The next sweep comes in a decade."

"Ten years!" exclaimed Levi. "Ten years of being out there! Duster might have died from who knows what danger by then. And what about Siv and Glass? Why were the other duplicates thrown out?"

"Who knows what reason Mal might use?" toned Celester. "But I would guess that after throwing out Duster, Mal came upon random Dusters who reminded It of the first. So in Its illogic It threw them out. The first Siv was thrown out for whatever infraction of Its rules, and the first Glass. Then others followed."

They could imagine Colossus sweeping in the light, as Mal swept in darkness.

"So you go about undoing what the Mal has done?" Justice said.

"It is so. Colossus saves humanity," Celester toned. "Yet, since the mistake Colossus made of sending Starters away, Mal evolved. It has existed ever since.

"By the way," Celester added, "it was Mutant II that Mal found misfit, not Mutant I. The first mutant was prototype for all developing Slakers. But Mutant II refused necessary time underground. It developed unseen movement, mind-control, to beat Mal and get to the surface. It developed flight for females only, when all must be the same here. It was thrown out."

Preoccupied, Justice said, "I wonder, Celester . . . Colossus says it knows no Mal. It's as if it has no idea what goes on when Mal is here."

"Better now to speak of other things," Celester toned, a harsh, discordant sound.

"Why doesn't Colossus stop Mal from throwing people out?" Dorian wanted to know.

"Colossus just kept saying, 'I know no Mal,' like that," Justice said.

"The Mal be—" Celester began, but did not finish.

"Do you suppose Mal might not know of Colossus either?" Levi said. "Would that make any kind of sense?"

"Oh . . . yes!" Justice said. The underground dimmed ever so slightly. She saw it happen, the only one of them besides Celester to be aware of it. She experienced that instant's premonition, like the painful prick of a thorn, sharp and quick.

Join! she traced in a breathtaking command. At once they locked thoughts that merged into one gripping mind concentrating on home. The glowing blue of insight, of power, rose in the mind.

i am the Watcher! was the unit joined. Their physical selves vanished.

"Mal is come," toned Celester in chilling minor chords.

Darkness. The unit was hurled helter-skelter. It was blown into blackest space. It lost Celester.

I am Mal! screamed Mal in an explosion of sound.

i am the Watcher!

The unit found itself in the Crossover between times. It concentrated on time/location—home.

Outcasts! raged Mal. *I will see you back and back. I warned you. I will follow you back and strike down all of your kind!*

The unit felt sick to death, spinning in darkness of Mal, which surrounded it.

i am the Watcher! The unit concentrated, but

it was not getting home. Its mind stretched and bended. That which was growing within fought to free itself.

Who are you? spoke the unit of its growing, changing self.

i am the Watcher. i . . . i . . .

I am Mal. You will go back and back! Darkness of Mal was a great weight on the unit mind.

All at once the unit was no longer in a writhing, plunging condition between times. It could not focus its power-of-being on the shade buckeye tree at the Quinella lands. The Crossover turbulence no longer echoed with sighs and whispers of mind-travelers come and gone.

What has happened? fleetingly the unit wondered.

Swarms of multi-beings hung still in space. They were like huge clouds of mites caught by an invisible stickiness. Everything had ground to a halt. The unit was stuck, with no power of mind to move whatever it moved to get to the present. All was still, except for the non-being of Mal.

Darkness of Mal twisted and turned upon itself and the unit. The non-moment and nowhere of Crossover was a shiny spiral through which Mal was a dark movement. Mal tried to split the unit apart. It attacked with ill-will and indifference.

The unit held on.

i am the Watcher. i know this place.

It held fast to this one thought that was clear: i know this place. This spiral of Crossover, the spring, the same silver coiling the Justice one spoke of. This is of Colossus. A connection of Colossus. Does Colossus know it is infested?

I KNOW, came to the unit.

Colossus, i am trapped in Crossover and cannot get home.

The spiral of Crossover straightened. It became a chamber. Within it was the unit suspended, and all t'beings suspended. Mal was outside the chamber. The unit saw It clearly, darkly, violently moving and whipping around the outside. The chamber was itself suspended within the Colossus complex, a single component of the miracle machine.

You are magic, spoke the unit. You are a marvel, Colossus.

I KNOW I AM MUCH, informed Colossus.

Can you see the Mal there, waiting to get to me again? spoke the unit.

MAL? I KNOW NOT OF IT, conveyed Colossus.

Celester materialized in the chamber and came toward the unit.

i am glad to see you, Celester, spoke the unit. i am trapped here in this nothing. See, out there is Mal. When i mention It to Colossus, Colossus repeats the same words.

"I am aware of this," toned Celester. "And I

stopped the Crossover because of this. You must understand that Colossus knows nothing of Mal."

You have not spoken of Mal to Colossus in all this time? spoke the unit.

"Colossus is while Mal is not," toned Celester. "Can you understand that?" His soundings were muted, yet no less marvelous in the stillness of Crossover. "Colossus cannot know of Mal. At the moment of Colossus' utter despair when it realized its mistake of sending Starters away, it fell to pieces. One piece was strong enough to emerge as a separate entity. An opposite entity to Colossus. That entity is Mal."

"Like Colossus it cannot be comprehended," toned Celester. "Colossus is here around us. Yet it knows nothing of Mal."

But Mal was in here, too, the unit persisted.

"Mal did not know where It was. And Colossus is not conscious of It."

i see, spoke the unit, and was quiet. A moment later, when it spoke again, it said, "This Crossover, the same as Colossus, must have been built by Starters also."

"Just so," toned Celester.

i do not know why Starters built it.

"It was long ago," toned Celester. "A bridge to all times. Starters built Colossus machine from genetic gifts. But one gift Starters could not uncover. Starters built bridge so that which Starters could not uncover might find its own way. Many minds came forward time after time, but none have come with the gift that fit."

Until now, spoke the unit.

"Yes, until now," agreed Celester.

For i have the gift.

"The final fitting of Colossus is within you," agreed Celester in harmonious tones. "The reason Colossus summoned me when I was showing you the domity."

Their memory informs me you would seem to turn off—is that when Colossus summoned you? spoke the unit.

"Yes, that was when," Celester toned. "Colossus said, '*They* are different from the other three with power.' By *they*, Colossus meant the Justice one. I did not comprehend at once when he spoke of her as *they*. And then I recalled seeing her Watcher power."

And then you knew, spoke the unit.

"I knew then," toned Celester. "The brothers are twinned. So, too, is the sister. Great Colossus reasoned that the evolving Watcher was the gift that would soon fit."

The Watcher grows to become free, spoke the unit.

"Just so," toned Celester. "Starter wisdom was great and godly."

Were they gods? spoke the unit.

"Gifts collected by Starters from seers to make Colossus machine are godly," Celester toned. "But now I must inform you," he toned more solemnly, "you will regress now in time, First Unit. You will go and you may never return."

The unit fell silent. It responded finally: i understand. i have brought the gift. It is almost ready to be free. But how will i return to my time frame without it?

"The Watcher will see you through the Crossover," toned Celester.

Yet i am caring about Duster and Miacis and the tribes of Dusters, Sivs and Glasses. And the grims, spoke the unit.

"Never fear," toned Celester. "What is best for them will be done."

There will be changes in domity? In Dustland?

"With Colossus complete, change is bound to occur. With the Watcher in place, Colossus alone will know what to expect. But the grand design must continue for a thousand years of Reclaimen. Perhaps work will be done on the outside as well as in domity. We have concentrated so hard on raising domity. Perhaps we have neglected study of the outside."

Will Starters be found and returned? spoke the unit.

"I suspect Starters have brought to being a

new world by this time," toned Celester. "Perhaps they search for us, to give us back . . . something of value." Humming, "One of the four will know answers to much upon the unit's return home."

You are a seer, too.

"All are seers who are Starters, or made by Starters," toned Celester.

Might i speak for the last time with Colossus?

"As you wish," toned Celester, stepping aside.

Colossus, i am returning home.

The Colossus emitted a sense of caring and understanding: GO THEN, FIRST UNIT.

i thought the destiny of the Justice one was the future. But i cannot come back, Celester says. i thought i would come and go as long as i wished.

The Colossus conveyed that the unit's destiny was to deliver the gift of the Watcher. For the Watcher was necessary for the completion of itself.

i know. Good-bye, Colossus.

The Colossus emitted a sense of profound spiritual closeness with the unit. FARE YOU WELL, FIRST AND LAST UNIT. GOOD-BYE FRIEND.

Celester stepped near First Unit again. He witnessed the many eyes pierced with glowing that lit the chamber of Crossover. He observed First Unit change and grow, as was necessary in this moment of final parting.

i did not speak good-bye to Duster or to Miacis, spoke the unit.

"Speak then, as you wish," toned Celester.

Miacis and Duster were translocated in the chamber. They appeared before the unit.

"Where you been, First Unit?" Miacis cried out. "My God, lady, what's going on?"

The unit laughed. It reached out with affection, mind-touching a good-bye.

"First Unit, you have to go?" Miacis asked.

Yes, and i will not see you again, Miacis. But i will remember you and cherish the memory.

"Oooh, I feel awful sad," cried Miacis. "But I'll stay with Duster and I'll be all right. Guess what, lady. I'm beginning to see things! Lots of pretty sights. Guess I'll be seeing most things soon now, just like all the gyldan, just like Duster and just everybody!"

So Miacis had been told by the glowing, moving, immense Star of the trench underdome.

i am so glad for you, Miacis, spoke First Unit. And then: Duster?

"Be me," toned Duster. He stood quietly. "Be you, one, two, three and one humans?" His voice was strong in its leader's mode.

Yes. i leave for the far past place, spoke First Unit. i cannot return here.

"Justice?" Duster toned. "Thomas . . . Lee . . ."

All are here, toned First Unit. Good-bye, Duster. Be well.

"Be going home to dust-time and pool. Be going with my smooth and leggens."

It will be good for you there, spoke the unit.

All at once the Crossover commenced its turbulence. The unit heard Duster call distantly, "Be tight, you!" He vanished, as did Miacis and Celester.

Be tight, you, Duster, Siv and Glass. The unit sent this tracing. *Celester?*

"I am standing by," toned Celester from far.

Good-bye. Good-bye, Celester, toned the unit. Thank you for all you taught the four.

"Good-bye, only unit of twentieth century," came the faint but pure toning.

The last time: i am the Watcher!

The Crossover swarmed and heaved. Mal was there in smothering darkness. The unit cried out against the fierceness of Mal, whose purpose was to keep misfits away from domity. The unit heard itself heaving for air, for Mal was ghastly and oppressive. The unit felt breathtaking stabs. It feared it would not have strength to beat Mal down and set itself free at the same time on the far side of Crossover.

Let go of me! warned the unit. It tasted sickening bile.

i am the Watcher!

Watcher was there, a blast of color in the center of Mal-dark. Light enclosed the unit in its care. Watcher fought Mal and guided the unit through.

I am Mal! spoke Mal, whipping its deep shade to taunt the light.

Careful, Mal, or i will turn you inside out, warned the Watcher.

Who dares speak to me in waves of light?

i. You will know me soon enough.

It was a splendid Watcher, growing more serene and powerful each second. All at once it exploded in billions of sparks, lighting up the black of Mal. Watcher burned holes through the dark to gather itself in one spectacular beam on the outside. Watcher surrounded Mal and pressed Mal on all sides.

Get away! cried Mal. *Hurting, get gone!*

The dark heated under burning pressure. It melted in a solid weight, was rounded, glowing with heat. Mal fought with Its sickness, but light knew no sickness.

Watcher heaved the unit far out of range of the glowing ball of Mal to keep it safe. Burning pressure the Watcher had fixed on Mal kept It heating and glowing. Mal became a solid weight, shining, hanging in the Crossover. T'beings swarmed over It, sensing weakness. They knew It had been a living entity. They thought that now It was quite dead. Hordes of them picked at the ball of Mal until Watcher came, singeing them in its light.

Not for you, Watcher informed them. When i am done, this Mal will be my treasure.

Watcher concentrated on knowing and observing and on getting the unit home. It steadied light-motion. It softly lit the unit's way through the nothing of no-time. For had not the unit performed well, a spaceship carrying the Watcher safely to its place?

i am the Watcher. Observing, surrounding the unit with utmost attention and clear purpose. So much did Watcher comprehend. It was light. Never did it not know.

For a non-moment it glowed especially in the Justice one, where it had waited, changing and growing all of this long time. Years in the genetic life of the child.

Then it was free!

i am the Watcher.

A wrenching pain sent the unit's mind reeling. Sparks flew, exploding on the unit; then, one by one, most of the sparks went out. They did not burn the unit. A measurable few remaining disappeared inside the unit. The unit thought such pain was Mal. It couldn't comprehend what was happening. It was so confused with pain, it thought Mal had struck a fatal blow.

i am dying.

Watcher, now free, left the unit on the seam between Crossover and the present.

Wait. The unit looked toward future for help. There it saw the sweetest blue light covering the darkest, shiniest ball. Light and dark retreated, blinking on and off, through Crossover's opposite end.

From the distance spoke the Watcher: You do not die so easily, First Unit. You who brought me safely to Colossus. Farewell, unit.

And far, far distant the grand, deep tone of Celester was humming in good humor.

The unit plunged from the seam.

12

There began the present. Thomas' eyes blinked rapidly. He thought he had been dreaming. Then he remembered everything all in a rush.

Must've been knocked unconscious, he thought. He saw the Quinella Trace lands he had known all his life.

We're here!

The lands teemed with life, shadowy and frisky. There was dusk of dawn wrapped around odors of decay. Overripe scents made his mouth fill with saliva. He managed to swallow, keeping his stomach down.

Am I by myself inside? With mental fingers and inward eyes he searched out every nook and cranny of his mind. He felt no other presence. But Justice still might be there. She knew how to get inside his head without him knowing.

Girl, if you're there, you'd better move out!

He turned his mind icy cold and laughed to himself.

I'm alone. No more First Unit. No more being scared to death in a place who knows how many thousands of years from now. Oh, man!

His hands commenced tingling.

Good, relax the fingers. Easier said than done. I can't move a muscle. Wait a little while. Take it easy.

He had been deaf to sound; now it overwhelmed him as indistinct noise. It took time for him to figure out that he had just heard his sister bursting into tears. She started crying like she intended going on forever; then stopped.

One of them cried, usually, on a return. The crying somehow released tension for all of them. But this was the first time Justice had cried.

I cried once, he remembered. Now I feel like laughing. Yeah. Home free! No more rope around my neck. I'm really, really home.

Dorian Jefferson faced away from the Quinella River toward the field of long grasses and weeds through which they passed to and from the Quinella lands. Beyond the field the Quinella Road twisted its way up the steep hill. He grew conscious of breathing deeply, squinting against bright sunlight. His eyes burned and watered, and he wished he could wipe them dry. He realized their hands were still joined, and that he had dreamed the sunlight. He closed his eyes to rest them and tried to get a picture of what had happened and how long ago. Then he sucked in his breath, remembering the great light and the ball of dark receding.

It's over! But does it mean—?

He didn't finish the thought. Impressions bombarded him; sights and sounds were so wonderful, they made him tremble. Incredibly, he was staring at a rabbit, having opened his eyes again just as it hopped from brown weeds some thirty yards away. He could see it clearly through the wild whips of branches growing out of the buckeye trunk. He was sure the rabbit didn't see him. They were very still under the tree. The rabbit sniffed and made a whistling sound, which astounded Dorian. He watched it until it disappeared in the weeds. If he could see the rabbit, then it was day. What he saw was vague light, the light that gathers ghostly before the dawn.

Then he thought of all the animals there were on earth. All the life! Future was *so* empty.

He could not feel his hands, but knew the weight of them locked tightly with Thomas' hand on one side of him and Levi's on the other.

He tried to speak, but his mouth wouldn't work. He kept trying; knew his mom would be around close by.

She doesn't even know we're back. How could she, unless she was looking into our eyes?

Mom? Mom! That's stupid, she can't hear you.

Dorian thought to send a healing aura out through his hands to the other three. He willed it to them the way he always did from someplace within that felt as though it existed behind his eyes. He willed the healant down his neck and shoulders and through his arms and hands. He waited for the warmth of giving that always came into his hands, but he felt nothing.

Levi thought someone was holding their hands in front of his face. It came to him that the hands were green. They weren't hands at all. What he saw were clusters of buckeye leaves spread out like fingers. They were lovely.

He stared, transfixed, seeing into his own mind. He became aware of things most astonishing.

With her back against the tree, Justice felt the weight of gravity. As she came to, she had the sensation of being pulled down and she could not move against the force. Her hands were gripped by Thomas' hand and Levi's. Soon she was able to think clearly. She started crying because she felt sad being home; then she felt glad, so she stopped crying. Tears blinded her. Once they dried, she saw Mrs. Jefferson just beyond the branches. Her back was to the tree. She was deep in thought, staring at the river, which looked black in the pale light. Warily Mrs. Jefferson glanced around at nearby beds of garter snakes. Here was where the snakes nested, lived and died. Heat had caused her dress to stick hotly to her, and she pulled at it and wiped the sweat from her neck.

Justice wondered why the Sensitive had not become aware of their presence. She watched as Mrs. Jefferson rubbed her knees. That was why—the rheumatism in her legs had filled her mind with pain. Softly, softly the Sensitive began singing in a throaty voice that got stronger as it went along:

"A-workin' in the field
A-wearin' my bandanna
Ol' sun were a woman
An' they call her Hannah
Oh, won't you go down, go down
Hannah, go down."

Justice listened, startled by the loving, long-ago race sound of it. The sun, a woman. Miacis had called the sun Star. Hannah was such a better name. When you got too tired in the fields, you asked Hannah and she would set herself down.

A husky voice broke in: "Mom. Mom, I'm home." Dorian had found his voice.

Mrs. Jefferson leaped up and spun around. Justice had never thought a woman her age could move so fast.

She's only a couple of years older than Mom, I bet. She just seems old. Being a Sensitive must make you old.

The Sensitive was beneath the branches. She looked into Justice's eyes.

"Child!" she exclaimed, touching her cheeks with gentle, knowing hands. Quickly she crawled around the tree and came back with Dorian, dragging him slung under her long arm like a sack of flour. She had unlocked his hands, and he was stretching his fingers to get the circulation working. She pried Justice's hands from Levi's and Thomas'. "Oh, my! You don't know how good it is! Yes! I never thought the day would come. I fixed my mind y'all might be gone another week. Happy birthday, Justice-chile. Yes, happy birthday to you!"

"Is it my birthday?" Justice whispered.

"Already past the time," the Sensitive said. "You still a year older, though, even if you missed the birthday."

"I'm twelve!" said Justice.

"But your mother . . ." Mrs. Jefferson stopped. Something.

The brothers were on opposite sides of the tree. Mrs. Jefferson could see only their profiles. They hadn't moved. There was something in their stillness.

She let Dorian gently down in the tight space

between Justice and Levi. She crawled around until she could see Levi's face. "How you doin', Number Two?" she said, smiling at him, looking into his eyes. She took his hands and rubbed them vigorously.

"Ow!" he said weakly, with a bit of humor at her enthusiasm. He did not smile exactly, but his face was calm. The depths of his eyes showed no sickness.

"I'm well, I think," he mumbled, his voice husky from the long silence. "I'm very well."

"Did they do it over there?" she asked. "Did *they* make you well?"

"Yes," he said. A vivid image of Sona, imagining he breathed the antiseptic, tranquilized air.

"Must be some place, over there," she said, but asked no questions. She would have the story from Dorian soon enough.

She moved over to Thomas. He had managed to turn his head so that he confronted her first. That was always his first concern, to be in control. He stared her down. Coldness. She would welcome him in any case, as she had the others.

"How you doin', Number One?" Clasping his hands in the warmth of hers, she felt his revulsion in a slight tremor in his fingers. She entered his mind smoothly, still smiling and without his knowing, as she could do even to one such as Justice. For she was the Sensitive, the bridge over deep waters. She was the tool and the divining instrument.

Thomas' mind was an elaborate weave of emotions and manners of acting that were hard to follow. She found his knotted obsession that he must be better than Justice. All of his many dislikes were exaggerated. Now that he was home, he had no fear.

She saw nothing about him that she had not already known. She kept her gaze steady on him, forcing him to respond to her greeting.

Stupid spirit woman! he thought. "I . . . I'm fu-fu-ine," he stammered, furious that only in the wretched future could he talk as he wished. "I'm fine, I'm fine!" he told himself, speaking beautifully in his head.

"Oh, that's good, Number One," Mrs. Jefferson said. "Y'all sure had a time, too."

She turned back to her son, crawled over to him. "Get y'all working again. Goodness! You as stiff as a board." She had Dorian by the shoulders. "Feel them muscles—just like rocks." Expertly she kneaded the trapezius muscles and deltoid muscles of the neck and shoulders. Oh, she knew muscles, all right. Soon Dorian felt pins sticking him all over.

"Oh, man!" he moaned.

"But you'll live," she said, laughing.

Justice touched her arm. "Mrs. Jefferson. Mrs.

Jefferson. It's . . . it's gone," she said, sounding as tired and apprehensive as she felt.

"Shhh, now," Mrs. Jefferson said, "don't you worry. We gone get y'all moving and we can talk tomorrow, or even next week. It's for sure you home now, and we got plenty of time."

All of them had their voices and could move their necks and arms and, clumsily, their legs, by the time Mrs. Jefferson had taken the last one of them in hand. Levi was standing, looking quite fit.

"It was the twilight of the breaking day when you come back," said the Sensitive. "See the sun-up coming!" Just then the sun winked over the horizon, lighting the trees, the field in a fresh yellow glow.

They drank in the clean brightness of the air. They could have cried, but Mrs. Jefferson wouldn't give them a sentimental moment.

"Come on, Dor," she said to her son. "Shoot, be gettin' on back before your daddy catch the house all empty." She was already walking away. She was beside herself with happiness to have the boy back, to have the three others back. But best to keep herself under control. No sense having a child break down by her example.

She stopped, turned back. Dorian, close behind her, almost ran into her; he stopped himself from bumping her by stepping quickly backward.

"Justice," she said. The child was there with her brother Levi, with Thomas off a way by himself. Wasn't that just like the Number One? "You all take your time," she said, with not a trace of Southern accent.

"What day is it?" Justice asked.

"Saturday," the Sensitive said. "You have been gone since Monday evening."

"Saturday," Justice said. Absently she touched her face. She looked down at her legs, her arms. She looked like her real self, no thinness anywhere.

"Justice," the Sensitive said, staring at the three of them, "Your father got into the habit of coming down here looking. I suggested to his mind that he not walk here, for fear he would be seen. People know he is a smart man. If they saw him by the river, they might think there was something to see here. So he never came in here, but he did sit there in his car a minute before going on. Maybe it was a comfort for him. You might see him this morning, although it is Saturday."

She moved away quickly with her son.

The three Douglasses went back to the river, careful of the snakes. There were lots and lots of snakes. The river was a sick river, black with algae and leeches.

Levi shivered, remembering that once leeches had got him.

No, it was Thomas who had the leeches all

over him, he thought. But, using his power, he made *me* feel the pain.

Thomas looked at the river with no feeling for it whatsoever. It just smelled foul and he turned his back on it.

Justice wished the river were clean, like the water pool they'd given to Dustland.

Why didn't we ever set our minds to cleaning up this place? she wondered. With all the power we had, we could have done it easily. We didn't think of it because we take everything for granted—what's one small stream when we have so much?

She sighed. "Shall we go?" she asked her brothers.

"St-st-stay a li-littttle l-l-longer," Thomas said.

"Yeah," Levi said.

Justice didn't want to go home quite yet either. They needed time to bring themselves completely back. Justice felt literally torn apart from her brothers and knew they must be feeling the same about her and each other. Each felt alone, separate, in a way they never had. She saw Thomas glance at Levi, then away uneasily.

Like we no longer know one another, Justice thought, gazing at Levi. How much older he seemed, but in a good way. His skin was clear and healthy-looking.

"You look just great," she told him.

"I feel great," he said. "I think I'll go get a check-up just to be sure."

"That's not a bad idea," she told him.

"Wwwant muh-muh-eee to-to sc-scan yyyou?" Thomas said.

"No, thanks," Levi said. He didn't want Thomas to invade him that way ever again. Then suddenly he stiffened, staring at Thomas. "You mean, you can still—" He could not finish.

"Oh, y-eah, I-I ffforrrrgot," Thomas said. "W-w-wow!" He blanched under Justice's careful gaze. "S-s-sorry."

They heard a car. There were not many cars on the Quinella Road early on a Saturday morning. This one did not slow down. With the overhanging trees, they could not see the car. They listened until it was beyond their hearing. A half-hour later another car came. This one slowed. They looked up. And then Thomas was racing to the field. Justice and Levi heard the car stop and Thomas yelling, "Dad! Here!" She and Levi hurried out. She was vaguely aware that Thomas had spoken two words without stuttering—a result of his excitement on seeing their dad, she supposed.

She gave a last glance to the sluggish Quinella River, then followed Levi through the field. She felt awkward, not knowing what to say to her father.

Will he let me just shake his hand?

Her dad was halfway out of the car, grabbing Levi by the head and shoulders in greeting. He must have greeted Thomas the same way.

He was staring at her. She touched her face, just to be sure, and stopped a few paces away from him.

"Hi, Dad," she said, her hands in the pockets of her jeans.

"Ticey!" He saw at once that she was older, taller. He reached out, pressed his hand on her curly hair. Precious Ticey! "I'm glad you're back," he said. Was it possible she had grown more than two inches in just five days? No, but over the whole summer it could happen. One would notice only if she were away for a time and returned. One would see the difference as he saw it now. Gently he kissed the top of her head as, shyly, she held her face away from him. He patted her shoulder. "Let's go home," he said. Looked all around. "I assume the boy and his mother have already gone." Caution in his voice.

"Yes," Levi said.

"Okay, pile in." They did, with Justice in front in the middle and Levi by the window. Thomas was in the back, surrounded by Mr. Douglass' stone-cutting tools.

Her head lolled on her dad's shoulder. It was wonderful being in the car, being close to her dad. She didn't say a word. None of them did.

Mr. Douglass almost said, "The town hasn't changed a bit since you've been gone." It went through his mind to say it seriously, as if they'd been gone a year.

I promised June they'd come back. I *knew* they would, he thought. No, you didn't know any such thing. Yes, you did. You knew their fighting spirit. Whatever it is, this power, you knew it would get them home—is that it? What has happened to them?

Something had affected them deeply. No chatter from them as there had been other times when they returned. Wisely he surmised that he and his wife would not know what it was for a while, if ever.

What does it matter? They're home!

They were at the top of the Quinella Road, where once, one rainy night, Justice had made a huge image of her own head and shoulders at least forty feet high. And with the moon caught in the tangles of her hair. Thomas had made the illusion of a McDonald's with the golden arches and an aroma of Big Macs.

What a night that was, she thought. It had been the time Mal had first come out of the future to warn them.

No more Mal. We gave up a lot to be free of it.

The next thing she knew, they were passing

under the great cottonwood tree at the entrance of their property.

Cottonwoman! "I thought the leaves would've changed!" she said, surprised that the leaves were still green.

"Me, too," said Levi.

Their dad said, "Well, it's still only August 1990."

"Wh-wh-wh—" Thomas couldn't get the word out.

The next minute they were all laughing.

"Dad, you nearly scared me to death!" Justice said, finally stopping.

"Oh, man, I believed it, too," Levi said.

"I'm glad it's not 1990," she said. "I've got a lot to do before then."

"What have you got to do?" Mr. Douglass asked, talking smoothly now with the kids.

"I don't know, but I know it's a lot," she said.

He laughed and eased the car up to the front of the house.

"Yey! Yey!" Justice said softly.

He turned off the motor and Mrs. Douglass came quickly out of the house to meet them.

13

She kissed and hugged each one of them, holding their hands, their faces, touching their hair, looking into their eyes. She liked what she saw. "Tice, you've grown!"

She would not pretend that nothing unusual was taking place or had occurred. She told them Mrs. Jefferson called to tell her they were back. She was frank and loving. "You all look different. I can't tell you how yet, but you are, I can tell. And that's good. Yes, I'm sure of it. Thomas, don't look so worried, I'm not going to cry. I promised myself I wouldn't. Oh boy, let's get inside before I get on my knees and pray!"

They grinned. Their mom was nice. She kept up a stream of talking, sensing that they were so grateful to be home, they wanted only to be silent, to be loved and have her fuss over them.

Inside, they went in and out of every room,

saving their own rooms until last. They picked up objects, turning them over and around as though they'd never seen such things in their lives. It took them most of the day to settle down, become used to living in a house again. They stayed together, not quite trusting their safety. At one point they found themselves in the laundry room, drawn there by an unusual absence of sound. For the first time in memory, they didn't hear the washer and dryer going.

"We've been gone long enough for all our clothes to be clean at once," Levi said.

Justice touched the machines. Machines! Differences of present and future stunned her.

The family sat down together around the kitchen table for breakfast. The three of them ate lightly. They would have to gradually get used to so much plenty. Afterward Justice went to her room and slept. The boys went to their room, too. She awoke much later feeling refreshed, calm, and she was able to take a good look at her room and herself in the mirror. Her room was so neat, not a trace of mess or dirt anywhere. Give me a few days, she thought lightly, and it'll look just like a tornado hit it.

She peered at her face in the long mirror on her wall. She touched it. It was her own self, looking the way she'd hoped she would look. She couldn't see any change of growing to twelve at all. And the elongated figure she had mysteriously become had disappeared without a trace.

Am I really me? she thought. Don't think too much about it today.

Her reflection gave her no cause for alarm. She went to the kitchen. Her mom and dad were outside somewhere. Her brothers were quiet, probably still sleeping. Justice listened, hearing her folks talking quietly. The windows were up on screens. There were sounds of scraping, perhaps digging. They were working in the garden, which was what they liked to do. It amazed her that present life had gone on, uninterrupted. No dust sifted through the windows!

The kitchen was a neat space before the next meal, with chairs pulled in at the table and all the cupboards closed, breakfast dishes done. She took the small pink radio from the counter. The radio had been pay for some job her dad had done somewhere for someone. She took it back to her room, plugged it in behind her bed and listened to music, let it wash over her. She held the radio up close to her ear so the music could shut out all other sounds. She shut her eyes, let the radio play all the tunes. She switched stations again and again to keep the music going.

It was time again to sit down to a meal. The food they consumed in one day, Justice thought, was enough to feed the packen plus Miacis for a week.

It was a good supper. Cheeseburgers—really big and flat, like at McDonald's—corn on the cob, green beans from the garden and salad. Just right. But more than enough. Sprite to drink. Justice would have preferred root beer, but the Sprite would do fine. They ate everything, feeling slightly guilty. They were polite and no nonsense about them, truly unlike themselves.

Mrs. Douglass kept talking. Mr. Douglass made jokes whenever there was a lull. Her parents were only trying to give them time—how did they know that she, especially, needed to grow into being twelve?

I haven't been twelve for very long. Oh, I'm sorry I missed my birthday.

At once she burst out with, "Well, what happened to my cake?"

Mrs. Douglass laughed. "I froze it so you'd have it."

"Well, I want it now!" she said, just like any old twelve-year-old, and they all laughed.

Thomas didn't laugh. She could tell. His mouth opened, his lips pulled back, showing teeth, but there was no laughter in his eyes. He wasn't even thinking about her. She could tell that, too. His mind wasn't with any of them but on something that had his full concentration.

They finished and she helped her mom and dad clear the table. It took about ten minutes to scrape and pile dishes and put things away. Clean up the crumbs.

Thomas and Levi slipped off while she was in the kitchen; she was glad to be with just her folks.

"Let's leave everything in the sink," her mom said.

"Yeah, and let's have cake!"

"In a minute," said her mom.

"Follow me," said her dad. Her dad took her mom's hand. Her mom took hold of her hand. Before Justice could get her wits about her, she was at the end of the line, being pulled through the house and on outside.

"Well, for . . . What is going on?"

"It's a parade," Mr. Douglass said.

"Hear the band?" her mom said when they were outside. They paused in the backyard, which was overgrown and wildly beautiful with planted beds of flowers and stubborn, blooming weeds that wouldn't die until winter. On the opposite side of the yard was her mom and dad's large vegetable garden, which, by the looks of it, was a complete success.

Justice heard a moaning drumroll and a strange click-clicking in time with it.

With a flourish, Mr. Douglass whipped out a

handkerchief and made a blindfold to cover her eyes.

"Well, for . . . What is going *on*?"

"Silence, please," said her mom. Her mom and dad led her between them, once her blindfold was in place.

"I know! We're going—"

She heard the gate open in the high wooden fence that separated the backyard from their open field. It squeaked closed behind them.

Oh, but she could tell when they were in the open field, all one acre and a half of it planted in Kentucky bluegrass. She could smell the grass, knew it had been freshly mowed. She heard the moaning, which grew louder—Thomas' kettle-drums, of course. And the click clicking—what on earth could that be?

The blindfold was slipped off.

"Ta-dahhh!" said her mom and dad. Everybody hollered and whistled and click-clicked their forks and spoons together. It was a grand party just for her. For *her*!

All the guys and some girls, too. The neighborhood kids. She saw Dorian.

"Hi! Hi, everybody!" she said.

They were singing "Happy Birthday" and Thomas was acting a fool in his favorite hat, but not so much that the attention was taken away from her. There was her cake in the middle of a long tablecloth spread on the ground. The cake had chocolate icing. There were two other tablecloths, and kids were sitting around them, with a paper plate and cup in front of everyone. The kids wore party hats. Justice saw everything in a rush.

Mrs. Douglass lit the candles and brought the cake to where Justice still stood beside her dad. Mr. Douglass conducted "Happy Birthday" to its final, resounding "POM POM-AH"—on the kettledrums—"to you!"

There was a hush as Justice took a deep breath and blew out every candle to wild applause. "Yay! Yay!" kids yelled. There were little cups of nuts and candy, and the kids were all having a good time. Well, who wouldn't, with brothers and a mom and dad like hers?

And Levi coming up, ceremoniously putting a gold-crown hat on her head.

"Don't anybody dare to spank me," Justice said. "Don't anybody dare!" And all the wildness of chasing her clear across and around the open field. To catch her and give her her birthday licks; and she outran everybody for about ten seconds, yelling her head off for them not to dare touch her. Then they all had hold of her and piled on her and held her down. They got their licks in, each and every one of them, all pulling their punches, with Mrs. Douglass standing over them, saying,

"Now, not too hard, boys. Girls, you're worse than the boys!" Justice knew, when they'd finished, she wouldn't sit down good for the rest of the day.

Everybody tore away and left her lying there on the ground in the bluegrass, looking up at a forever sky, the kind her dad said was a California sky. It was a forever blue sky of no moisture, with just little sleeping puppies of clouds. Her dad said the sky and clouds arrived in Ohio country from westward by hopping a dawn freight train of the B&O Railroad.

"It's hotter'n hell," she cussed. "Boy, do I love this sunshine Saturday!"

Then she was up and on her feet. "Ow," holding her behind. "Ooooh, too many of you all!" She stood a moment. The field was twice as big in the growing shade. She was close to that part bordering on the backyards of Dayton Street. She saw Dorian Jefferson's yard with its low hedge. She wondered about his mom. "Bring her some cake tomorrow," she told herself. "Don't give any to Dorian to take home, I want to do it."

She drank in the sight of the dark green hedgerow, thorny and ancient, twisted by hard weather. The hedgerow bordered the whole of the west property line. She loved the old trees; and spun around to see her favorite cottonwood tree across the field from the hedgerow.

The hedgerow, the cottonwood, the sky and

land began to pulse and echo, and the very light of day was broken to pieces. Thomas' drumming rolled out of the trees to hit her between the eyes.

"Oh!" she said as everybody called her to come back. Everyone sat around the tablecloths again. She saw they had cake on their plates as she came up, feeling like a fool to have become dazed in the head out there where everybody could see how dumb-crazy she could get.

Mrs. Douglass' heart had sunk when suddenly Justice had stood so utterly still. A terrible fear had welled up. Mrs. Douglass thought maybe something—the Mal, they called it—had come out of the future. Or that Justice's power was taking her over. She would have sworn that her children had come back exactly like themselves inside, with nothing of that other part of them—she wouldn't allow herself even to think what it was for fear that by naming it she would somehow summon it. Her children had come home the way she'd raised them. Oh, they were changed, maturing. Wasn't it odd how you noticed it all at once? But they were her own children now. She would make home the best place in the world in order to keep them. She didn't know what she could do differently, but she would not even think about them leaving again.

There was a pile of presents next to what was

left of the cake. "Well, for . . . My goodness!" Justice exclaimed.

"You have to sit at the head," Levi told her. He was at one side of the longest tablecloth, with the presents in front of him. "I'll toss 'em to you."

She caught the first present and opened it. It was a nice card with a dollar bill in it from their friend Slick Peru. There were lots of cards with dollars in them. And she read all the cards out loud so everybody could feel proud. There was a pretty mother-of-pearl comb from Susie Mettfer. All of the presents were nice little gifts. She would have been embarrassed if anyone had given her too much. Nothing from her folks. They would wait until later, when all the kids had gone home.

Oh, boy! she thought, and opened a thin envelope that had written across it in ink, "From Your Big Brothers, Tom-Tom and Levi."

It was a book of certificates. "Well, I'll be!" She couldn't believe it. "Gift certificates, fifty cents each," she said, and flipped through the booklet. "A whole five dollars' worth of McDonald's!" They'd done this while she slept.

"All the Big Macs you can eat," Levi said. Thomas' drums gave rolling POM-AH POM-AH'S.

Justice giggled with glee. "Five whole dollars!" And laughed her head off, remembering the golden-arches illusion Thomas had made. She slapped the book a couple of times to make sure it was real. "Will the Big Macs *melt* in my mouth?" she asked her brothers, and winked outrageously, making sure they got her drift.

Levi grinned knowingly. Thomas listened to her with his head cocked to one side. He would glance at her, then away. Their eyes steadied on one another. Thomas was sure different today, she thought. Almost being nice. At least, he wasn't being mean. They held the look a moment, but made no certain contact with each other. It was like feeling couldn't come across between them.

Well, you can't have everything on your non-birthday, Justice thought.

Her mom and dad brought out three flavors of ice cream and stuff to drink. Everybody got served and sat and ate, except Thomas, who preferred standing off by his drums. He ate slowly but steadily. Justice knew the moment he felt her watching him. She had a smile all ready, but he did not look up. He paused, fork not moving, then continued eating.

"We're glad you're back," Talley Williams told her. Justice couldn't believe he'd said that until she realized it must have been suggested, when they didn't come back in a day or two, that they were on a trip of some kind.

But where did Mrs. Jefferson say we went? she wondered.

"Did you like the *Grand Canyon?*" Dorian said pointedly.

"Oh . . . oh, yes, we had a great time," she said.

The party had to end. After the food was gone, kids drifted away. There would be no games with Thomas. After all, it was Justice's birthday. A girl, Mary Lynn Logan, hung around Thomas. He kept playing his drums, but he gave her a look. It wasn't a mean look, Justice noticed. It was piercing. A swift, hard look of interest.

Well, I'll be! Justice thought.

Thomas wore his favorite hat, a purple toque with a large pink ostrich feather stuck in the band. He wore it like a prince. Imperiously, he stared Mary Lynn Logan down.

She was older than Justice, fourteen and some months. She lived in the neighborhood, loved to swim and once in a while rode bikes with Justice, if Justice could catch her on the street riding her bike. Mary Lynn stood there awash in Thomas' gaze, blushing to the roots of her long, dark hair.

Justice felt a hot downdraft of air from the treetops. It caused her tangled curls to spring up around her ears. High up in the trees there was a wind sigh, just like the sound of crowds ah-ing from a long way away. For a split second she had the notion, as did Thomas and Levi at about the same time, that out of the ah-ing sound the Mal would come sweeping. It was the time of day for It, and the moment when It was the farthest from their thoughts. Yet they had thought of It. But there came no inkling of forces from beyond. And no threat came. They were alone and safe. They waited a moment longer, but they were still safe.

Thomas broke the spell by adjusting his hat to the proper angle, peering at Levi, his mirror.

Mary Lynn laughed at them, they were so alike. Then she was startled when she happened to think about the endless reflections the brothers must have of one another.

Thomas laid the four felt-tipped kettledrum mallets carefully on the calfskin drumheads. He passed Mary Lynn and sauntered down the field. A little way and he turned around to walk backward, hands in his pockets. His look beckoned her. "I'll walk you home," he was saying without uttering a word. Quickly, head down, Mary Lynn followed.

"Well, well, well, *well*," Levi whispered in Justice's ear.

Justice had to cover her mouth and jump up and down to keep from whooping out loud.

Thomas and Mary Lynn Logan. "Do you *believe* that?" she whispered back. She had never once thought of Thomas in terms of *girls*. Levi, sure. But Thomas? Well, the world had to turn.

They cleaned up the field, collecting paper

plates and cups, plastic spoons and forks and soiled tablecloths, she and Levi working silently together. They were close now, as they had been ever since they'd come back. It was a different, respectful closeness after all they'd been through. Sunlight sparkled at them from behind the hedgerow. Shadows lengthened as they went back and forth.

"It was a good party," she said. "A swell party."

"A good and swell party," he said, making light. He gave her an affectionate bonk on the head.

"You can go on in," he said. "I'll wait for him and help with the kettles."

"Right," she said. "Aren't you glad we're here?"

"Yeah, but I still can't believe it," he said. "I had my doubts we'd ever make it."

"Me, too," she said. "But now I'm going to let things take care of themselves. I wanted . . . wanted you to know that."

"Justice, I know. I understand."

He did know. Knew everything she was trying to say without saying it, quite. Even he wouldn't say the exact words on this perfectly ordinary summer day. It could be the last one they would have. He was positive it was the final day that some part of them would enjoy doing the same things—Levi assisting Thomas in everything; Justice just plain old happy to be a part of their world.

"It's all going to change, Justice," he told her.

She listened to him, hardly breathing. His face wore an expression she had never before seen.

"I am the one who knows," he said.

"You're the one . . ." Her voice trailed off as she groped to remember.

"Celester," he said. "I'm the one he gave answers to about what will happen beyond."

She could see the astonishment of knowing in his eyes. And he sat down near Thomas' drums to wait for his brother.

Not today, she thought. I don't want to know. She turned and went through the gate to the house.

14

Thomas' feet pressed up against the underside of Levi's bunk above him. His hands were locked behind his head. He was out of the covers, wearing cut-off pajama bottoms, and he was relaxed, as though he had on a bathing suit and was lying on a riverbank somewhere taking his ease in the sun. It was deep in the night and everyone was asleep except him. He was wide awake in the dark and grinning from ear to ear. Every now and then he boxed the black air in front of him, punching it down, patting it up and knocking it down again. He began laughing so hard without making a sound that he thought he was going to choke. Made his side ache so bad he had to give some time to kneading it until the pain went away.

He had a slight apprehension that if he were too gleeful, something might come get him in the night. But he really did feel safe at home. He was positive the Watcher had got the Mal. So what could harm him? He just had to make a decision, was all. He grinned again. What was nice was that every time he opened his mouth he got another chance to decide.

Maybe it's supposed to be a punishment, he thought. Well, I think it's a real riot!

He pressed his feet as hard as he could on the bunk above, pushing in between the slats until he made Levi stir. And he said out loud, but very quietly and distinctly: "Brother mine, brother mine! How can you sleep with so much going on?" No stutter anywhere.

Levi stirred again; he said, "Huh?" Thomas could tell he never woke up. Levi thought he had been dreaming, probably.

Thomas smiled and lay still a few more minutes. Then he got out of bed and stealthily made his way to the living room. In the farthest corner by the windows he sat himself down with his legs drawn up.

Anybody see me like this will think I'm a looney tune, he thought.

The house wasn't dark at all. There was moonlight making the outdoors look like a still and secret kind of day. Thomas pulled back the curtain to get a better look. It was the truth, moonlight was *weird*—spooky the way it gave everything an unnatural intensity. He wouldn't have been shocked out of his head to see a bunch of zombies going to a blood-sucking in the hedgerow. On his knees now to see better, he stared a few minutes longer, just daring the glowing moon and the shadowy trees to give up some kind of death-dealing terror.

What would you do if something awful did come walking along? I mean, suppose this is judgment night and the dead folks get up to take a stroll. Thomas the ghoul. Did you forget what you came out here for?

He leaned back in the corner and in as ordinary and quiet a manner as he could manage, he commenced talking out loud.

"My name is Thomas . . . Douglass." Sometimes it was necessary for him to pause between words. It helped also when he spoke slowly and matter-of-factly. But in order to do that, he had to clean it up inside. Empty himself of—well, you might call it aggression. Meanness.

Tell the truth, he thought. You look at things and understand what's going on. You don't hate anyone for no reason or try to hurt anyone. Then —*you do not stutter.*

"Now, that takes the cake . . . d-d-don't it?" he said. Oh-oh. I had some anger there. He closed his eyes, trying to turn around whatever ugly thought he was going to think when he stuttered the word. He had to smile. It was so-o-o funny! His stutter was gone if he did not do harm to anyone else.

What do you mean, do! Even think it.

"That's it," he said softly. "All I have to do is find a way around it."

His mouth clamped shut. He couldn't open his jaws. He could barely swallow.

Thomas began breathing hard. He tried to swallow. It was as if something not only had its hand over his mouth but gripped him on the inside as well. The back of his mouth filled with saliva. His teeth were clenched shut. Fear flowed up his back and the saliva dried up. Suddenly the living room terrified him. What was happening to him? He knew. He knew!

I didn't mean it!—hands over his face, whimpering into his hands. He still couldn't open his jaws. Yes, I did mean it. I thought I could be smart and get around the conditions. You can't get around them, right? You do what's expected or you stutter, or you don't talk. Well, each time I'm just going to have to decide. There, now that's the truth. You can't expect me to be perfect every time. I'm working on it! But she isn't perfect either. Don't I have some rights, too? They say I never started stuttering until she was born. You figure it out. I don't know who said that, I don't remember.

"But it's a fact," he said out loud. He could talk. And he wasn't stuttering.

He smiled. "I wish I knew who I'm talking to or if I'm . . . talking to . . . anyone."

He could look at the room again and not be afraid. It was full of moonlight. Chairs, the couch, end tables, all swimming in moonglow.

"I'm . . . not talking to anyone. There's . . . no one here," he said, slow and easy.

"I think the spaceship must have . . . done it," he said. "When I asked if I could go . . . in space, it knew . . . why. Colossus is responsible. So what should I say?"

He knew what was expected of him, but that didn't make it any easier to say it. Maybe it was one of the conditions, having to say it.

"Thanks. You don't . . . know how grateful . . . I am for this. To be able to . . . talk. Well, it's a new experience. I haven't told anyone. It's too good. I wanted . . . to make sure in case . . . in case it vanished. When Levi tried to talk to me . . . yesterday, I'd think he was a jerk and that made me stutter. So he wouldn't find out. And Mom and Dad, too. I thought mean and so I stuttered at them. And I stayed out of her way for fear . . . but if I think about *her*, it opens a whole can of worms. So I leave it alone."

Silently Thomas got up and went back to his

room. Levi was deep asleep. Thomas got back into bed. No one had seen or heard him moving around. He listened, but all was quiet. He let his mind loose to roam over things.

Deep in the night, Justice woke up violently. She wasn't only a little startled. She had been lying on her back and she lurched forward, almost hitting her forehead on her knees. The waking up hit her like an explosion and she was gasping for air. In her arms she had three new paperback books her parents had given her. How did they get there? she wondered as they slid to the floor.

Justice fell back on the bed and pressed her hand to her chest. She saw the moonlight. It shone on the new birthday clothes hanging in her closet. It took time for her to get hold of herself. And she lay very still, until her breath was even. That had been a bad one. She remembered no dream, but she knew it must have been a bad one. Probably the whole business of getting back to the present and being scared and everything had caused it.

Funny how you dream bad when all the badness has passed. But it's good to get it out of your system, she thought.

So she went back to sleep. An hour later she awoke just as violently. Only this time she was standing in the moonlight, facing the closet. She had on the new jacket her mom had got her for school. As she awoke, she staggered and was terrified and for a moment thought she was back in the Crossover. She began to cry, making no sound. She took off the jacket and hung it up, crying. She was afraid to turn around, the moonlight was so bright. She didn't know what the moonlight had to do with anything, but she was afraid of it. She stepped into the closet and put her arms around her clothes. And cried. When the crying stopped, she just stood there. And when she was able to turn around, she kept her sights on her pillow, like it was a safe harbor in a storm. She scooted into bed and lay on her stomach, holding on to the sides of the bed. She was exhausted; that was why she fell asleep again.

She awoke violently the third time, still holding on to the mattress. Something. She didn't dare look around. But when she dared to look fifteen minutes later, there was nothing. Just moonlight. Why must it be so bright? She put the pillow over her head and made certain no part of her was sticking out of the covers. She breathed from a stream of air which followed a passage to her under the pillow. She was soon very hot, but she didn't dare take the covers off. This was how she fell asleep. When she awoke the last time, no less violently, she was on the floor. She had a dull headache over one eye and jumping nerves made her shake all over.

She didn't breathe hard or have any discomfort

except for the dull aching. She lay there, getting hold of herself.

Oh, man. Oh, my God, she thought.

But that was all. She got up and washed and dressed without waking a soul. It was seven forty-five and Sunday, and the house was still sleeping. She went into the kitchen, took what was left of the birthday cake out of the refrigerator. There was enough left for four nice pieces. She wrapped all of it in Glad-Wrap and a few white napkins to make it look more festive. She wouldn't be able to go over to Mrs. Jefferson's house until after eight-thirty, but she had to get out of the house now. She found a large paper bag from Kroger's and she put the cake on a paper plate and placed the whole thing at the bottom of the sack.

There, she thought, I can ride and not spill it. She'd have to ride with one hand, for she had no basket on her bike.

She got out of the house with no trouble. She got on the sweet bike and headed out. Nice being on her own so early in the day. Sundays in summer were as quiet as Saturday in the dead of winter when folks couldn't bring themselves out in the snow. On summer Sundays it seemed the whole town slept late or stayed in, getting ready for church. Not a soul. But she would go over to Mrs. Jefferson's about nine. Mr. Jefferson would be outside, washing his car. Always was on Sunday, getting the car ready for whatever they might decide to do.

She went straight south to the edge of town, then east to that edge where she hit Morrey Street going south to the railroad tracks. She paused at the top of the Quinella Road.

Do I want to go down there and have to ride all the way back up? I haven't even eaten anything. I could eat the cake. She stood undecided on the side of the road with her bike balanced between her legs. She opened the sack, but decided she wouldn't touch the cake and mess up the wrapping. She would go hungry. And she wouldn't ride down the Quinella and have to sweat herself all the way back up.

She set the sack on the road a moment and rested her head on the handlebars.

I'm blue, she thought. My head hurts me.

She was sad and tight as a drum inside. All the little nervous jumps were causing a bad taste of fear in her mouth, making her almost sick.

I got to go.

She picked up the sack and turned back, north along Morrey. By the time she got downtown and could read the clock on the bank, it was near enough to nine for her to make her way. She backtracked south up Xenia Avenue, then west on South College Street to Enon Road. There she rode around the High School grounds a while and the

Middle School grounds. This year she would be in Seventh Grade at the Middle School.

Seventh is nothing, she thought. Wish I was in Eighth or back in Sixth. Seventh is a hard nothing.

Justice didn't feel right. She felt downhearted and numb and sick and sad. But numb was most of it, and it got her upset.

She glided over to Dayton Street and came on from the westward end. That way she didn't have to go near the corner of Union, which was almost where she lived.

She tooled up the walk and made a left turn into the Jefferson yard. A hedge as tall as she was closed her off from the street. The Jefferson car was parked in the driveway on the right of the small lawn. Mr. Buford Jefferson and his only son, Dorian, were washing the car. White suds slid down the car windows and hood and fenders. She'd never known people to take care of a car so much. Care like a baby.

They looked up as she let her bike down to lie on the ground, the back wheel spinning.

"Hi, Justice," Dorian said. He gave a quick glance at his dad.

"Hi, Dorian. Hello, Mr. Jefferson."

Jefferson nodded, went back to his work. He wasn't the friendliest father in the neighborhood. Suddenly Justice wondered how in the world Mrs.

Jefferson had covered for Dorian the times they'd gone to the future.

You know how she did it, Justice thought. And it must be awful having to muddle folks' heads all the time.

"Is your mother at home?" she asked Dorian. "I brought her and you all some of my birthday cake." She spoke as sweetly as she knew how for Mr. Jefferson's benefit. But if she hoped to gain points by being a generous neighbor, she was wasting her time.

"I don't eat cake," said Jefferson.

Well, blip and bleep on you, too, old dude! she thought. She knocked and heard Mrs. Jefferson call come in. She turned the knob of the screen door and went in. She didn't bother noticing the picture window, which had always impressed her. It was like an oversized fish tank, like the kind they had in aquariums—glass set right in the boards of the house.

There was another world where the Jeffersons lived. Mrs. Jefferson was the owner of it. A short-handled broom leaned against the wall just inside the door. Justice looked at it and knew she had once swept the Jefferson walk with it. She couldn't remember right now why she had, or whether she'd got paid for it. What did it matter, anyway?

There wasn't a hallway inside the door. She stepped right in and was in the evergreen-carpeted living room, looking at walls painted cabbage green. There were no pictures. A floor-to-ceiling mirror gave back her reflection. There were pots and pots of green growing things. The plants held heat and made the place feel uncomfortably damp. Justice brushed by them.

"Mrs. Jefferson?" she called, going toward the back of the house. She found the Sensitive seated at the table in the kitchen, drinking coffee and reading the Sunday paper. Justice could smell pancakes. She looked at the oven. Leona Jefferson stood up and got the pancakes out of the oven. She put three nice-sized ones on a plate and sprinkled powdered sugar on them and then some butter, and poured syrup atop it all. She set the plate in front of Justice, along with a napkin and a knife and fork. Justice sat down.

"Milk or coffee?" the Sensitive asked.

Softly Justice said, "Milk." She gazed at Mrs. Jefferson's face. She loved that face. Knew it like she knew her own insides.

Justice ate and drank like she wouldn't stop. She ate everything and after, ran a finger across the plate just to get the last of the syrup. Mrs. Jefferson sat next to her. She wasn't reading the paper. She was waiting.

Justice pushed the empty plate out of the way. "Oh, wait," she said. "Forgot what I brought you." The sack of cake was on the floor at her feet.

"Here." She handed over the sack. Mrs. Jefferson did not look at it. She nodded thanks and set the sack on the chair next to her.

"So," Mrs. Jefferson said.

"So," Justice said. "It's not over. Is it?"

The Sensitive kept quiet, waiting.

"I thought it was all gone," Justice said. "I didn't try to trace or telepath or anything because I was so certain that with the Watcher gone . . . But last night! I kept waking up so scared. Something was right there, within me."

"Who have you told?" asked the Sensitive.

"Nobody," Justice said. "No one but you."

"Good. And no, it's not over," the Sensitive said. "I knew that the moment I saw your eyes when you came back. Listen, you must understand that you are gifted and the given don't disappear."

"But . . . but the Watcher."

"It's gone, yes. But you still got the makeup, haven't you—what you were born with?"

"You mean, my genes."

"Yes. And so, think of an eye and crying and a great tear filling and filling until it fall from the eye and roll down, it so full."

"What?"

"Justice, that's what it is. A filling up, slowly and ever so slowly until it fills up its place. And it becomes so full up, it has to fall or roll or *rise*."

"You mean, I'm to have the Watcher again?"

"Maybe not the same thing. Who knows how it will form? But it will be power. You will have to be prepared for it. And I will help you just the way I did help you the first time."

Justice shook her head. Her headache was gone, she realized, probably because she had eaten. A hungry headache, her mom called it. There was no point in her saying she didn't want power.

Mrs. Jefferson put her hand on Justice's shoulder, patted it. "Nothing for you to fear," she said. "It will take a long, long time, long as the Watcher taken. And by then you'll be older. So will Dorian and a better healer, too. And maybe I will know more and find the best way for you to learn the control of it."

"But what will I do with it this time?" Justice asked. "I can't go back to the future, can I?"

"I believe you will do like you did the first time," said the Sensitive. "It will transmit the need and you will accept the transmission. You will do whatever you find you must do. So let it alone. You don't need to worry about it."

"I won't, then," Justice said.

She sat at the table a while longer. Mrs. Jefferson got a phone call. It was Justice's mom.

"She's here," Mrs. Jefferson said. "Brought me some real nice cake. Sure was good, too. You make it, honey? I'll send her on home in a fast minute."

Justice smiled. "You haven't even seen the cake."

"Just a little fib. Don't have to see it. I know Dorian's going to be real happy to have an extra piece of it."

Justice got up. "Thanks for the breakfast. Those pancakes were *real* good!"

"Glad you liked them. You want this sack back?" She took out the cake, unwrapped it and stuck her little finger in the frosting. Licked her finger. "Uuum! That'll be nice for after my supper tonight."

Justice left by the back door because she felt like it. Mrs. Jefferson saw her out.

"Tell Dorian I left my bike and he can bring it over later, if he wants."

"Sure," Mrs. Jefferson said. "Justice, I told your mother you were coming home."

"Well, I am," Justice said.

She left and went into the field and strolled and dawdled inside the hedgerow, taking her sweet time.

At a quarter past eight Mrs. Douglass walked by Thomas and Levi's room and Thomas snagged her and woke his brother.

"Hey, Mom," he called through the door, "what's fer breakfast? Can . . . I have ham . . . and eggs?"

There was a long silence on the other side of the door. The door opened; Levi jumped down from the top bunk. He stood next to his mom and they both stared at Thomas as though they'd never seen him before. Mr. Douglass came in behind them, having heard Thomas' loud, unstuttered call.

Thomas kept his face straight for about five seconds; then he burst out laughing.

"It's true!" he said, grabbing pants to put on. "I came back . . . with it. I mean, I came back . . . without it. . . . I don't have to . . . stutter if I speak slowly and . . . relax myself." He did not mention the conditions. He hadn't lied or felt nasty toward anyone and his jaw didn't lock.

"Somehow they fixed it?" Mr. Douglass said, looking alarmed.

"I think they did," said Thomas. "Just the way . . . they gave that dog . . . Miacis her sight back."

"Maybe you'd better sit down and tell us everything now," Mr. Douglass said.

They started talking, thinking Justice was still asleep. Mrs. Douglass prepared ham and eggs. When she noticed the cake was gone, she knew that Justice was not in her room as she had thought all along. But she held off calling the Jeffersons in order to listen to the boys.

Thomas told about everything from the time they discovered Duster to the time they came back through the Crossover. It took him about fifteen minutes and he didn't stutter once.

"You really are safe," Mrs. Douglass said. Her eyes shone at them. "You don't ever have to go back."

"So it goes on and on over there right while we're sitting here," Mr. Douglass said. "It's funny how I think of it as *over there*, like it was another town."

"I think of it as beyond," said Levi.

"So . . . do I," said Thomas.

"I wonder what will happen when the Watcher is fitted in," said Mrs. Douglass.

Thomas was staring at Levi, for his brother had the oddest expression.

"You know, don't you, Levi?" He didn't take his eyes off his brother.

"I know some of it," Levi said.

"Really!" said his dad. "Well, let's hear it."

"I can't do that," he said. "I mean, it's not my way. See, Dad, you really have to 'see' the Slaker domity to appreciate it. You have to see the whole process of change. Hear Colossus explain by the displays how the large concentration of machines too close to the outer perimeter of the domity caused the magnetic roller storms and the heating up of the dust in Dustland."

They waited for him to go on. He was clearly excited, even inspired by it. But he would not go on. "I'll put it on paper." He smiled. He felt peaceful.

"Is that what you want to do?" his mom said.

"It's the only way I can really see it," he said.

They finished breakfast and Thomas went back to his room. He felt like playing his drums before he got into the shower, and he did play them. Levi stayed with his mom and dad, helping in the kitchen. He told her when it was time to call Justice.

"There's nothing to worry about. Mrs. Jefferson isn't going to hurt her or anything," he told them.

"Even so, I want her right here where I can see her," Mrs. Douglass said, and picked up the phone.

Thomas played, feeling the rhythms clear to his toes, letting his mind roam free.

Later Levi could hardly contain his excitement. He was filling up with knowledge that Celester—Colossus—had said one of them would have on their return.

I suppose it's just now all becoming conscious, Levi thought, although it sure feels as if my brain were filling up.

He went to the screened-in porch facing the front yard. It was a good place to sit and work out some things on paper.

Why did they want one of us to know things? he wondered. Maybe because they're rather lonely, isolated there. I mean, supposing you had an experiment going that included what was left of a once teeming world and you had to protect the experiment at all cost. The domity. Maybe it would feel good just to know someone outside knew. I'm amazed they were actually friendly. Pretty darn open, considering how alone they are. Oh, but that Colossus. How great a system it is! Oh, bless it for making me well again!

His hand trembled slightly as he began drawing a crude sketch of things he was beginning to know. It was the first of many, many sketches. He drew the way the Watcher fitted and the way it looked inside the silver coiling that was Justice's vision of Colossus, a true vision. The Watcher was a rod of fuzzy, soft-blue light. The light flowed into the coils, illuminating complex dimensions of Colossus. A beautiful, perfectly round diamond crystal larger than a basketball balanced at one end of the Watcher rod of light.

Levi sucked in his breath in stunned surprise. The crystal light pulsated on and off, generating perpetual energy. Levi knew it had been the round, dark ball of Mal before Watcher power had transformed it into Watcher treasure.

With all its parts, Colossus can do anything, Levi thought. Think of it! No more Mal to throw people out. All that live can be placed in domities—but slowly, so as not to upset the balance of things. And only if they want to come. Like Duster, many will stay in the open. So reclaim some of the open, why not?

Colossus had immediate transference through dimensions of time and space. Levi drew and drew. He drew Starters and amazing worlds. He drew Duster and Glass holding close, and a number of their offspring.

Puzzling aspects of future experiences became clear. He understood that because of the Watcher's power, the unit had passed through the Crossover and arrived beyond the domity of Sona, where it should have phased in. Instead, the unit had entered Dustland.

That's the reason Celester was so interested in us, he thought. We came from the wrong place!

He grinned in amazement as he realized that Celester had thought they were Starters! Then, with Colossus' interest, the discovery of the Watcher, the gift, was made.

How did we get our bodies in Dustland when nobody knew we were there?

At once he knew. The machines at the edge of domity, close to Dustland, which had affected the dust, also produced bodies, just as they did in domity.

We were lucky, he thought. Lucky we found Sona. But the Watcher had to find its way. Nothing was chance. Justice had to go to the future, bring the Watcher.

He drew and drew and was satisfied with his beginning. But it would take much longer to put what he knew into words. It would be more difficult. He leaned back, resting. He didn't have his strength back completely. He tired quickly, but he was well; he knew he was, and growing stronger by the hour. After a few minutes he bent forward again and carefully wrote notes to himself in the margins of his drawings.

It was lovely in the hedgerow this time of day. Full of shade. The smell of moss was pungent green and damp. Low limbs of the trees reached across the row, three feet above the ground, searching for sunlight. Justice sat on the limbs and made them bounce. She walked in the stillness; being in close contact with the osage trees took the heavy weight off her.

Why me? she wondered. Why is power forever mine? Chance, she answered herself. A roll of the dice. Power is my destiny. And my destiny is wherever power leads me.

That's it, then, she thought, and felt a little more accepting of her fate.

Now she could see her house through the branches. All around her she sensed a presence.

It was her own extrasensory she felt unsettling the air near her, and she toned down her thinking.

Once, not too long ago, she had hidden herself in this very same hedgerow from Thomas' presence searching for her. But that was past, done with, before she had become aware of her own presence. Now what she sensed was only herself.

Accept it, she thought. And she began to walk in tune with her unusual energy.

She continued on home slowly, easily. Her mind felt natural again. She sat down on a limb one last time before going in. Made it bounce with her, up and down, up and down.

Oh, enjoy it. I do love everything! she thought.

She felt coolness seem to rise from within the weeds, deep in the fresh, dark ground. She waited, calm, breathing in the goodness of the day.

Then she went on inside the house. Heard her brother drumming. Found her mom and dad.

About This Point Signature Author

VIRGINIA HAMILTON is one of the most distinguished writers of our time. Winner of the National Book Award and the Hans Christian Andersen Medal, she is the author of *M. C. Higgins, the Great*, winner of the Newbery Medal, as well as *Sweet Whispers, Brother Rush*; *The Planet of Junior Brown*; and *In the Beginning*, all Newbery Honor Books. Her books of folklore include *The People Could Fly*, winner of the Coretta Scott King Award; and *Many Thousand Gone*. Ms. Hamilton has also written the novel *Plain City*, an ALA Notable Book and a *School Library Journal* Best Book; *Jaguarundi*, a picture book; *Her Stories: African American Folktales, Fairy Tales, and True Tales*, winner of the Coretta Scott King Award, an ALA Notable Book, a BBYA, a *Booklist* Editors' Choice, a *School Library Journal* Best Book of the Year, and an NCTE Notable Children's Book in the Language Arts; and *When Birds Could Talk and Bats Could Sing*, a *School Library Journal* Best Book of the Year, an American Bookseller Pick of the Lists, an ALA Notable Book, and a BCCB Blue Ribbon Book. Most recently she is the author of *A Ring of Tricksters: Animal Tales from America, the West Indies, and Africa*. She has been awarded the 1995 Laura Ingalls Wilder Medal as well as honorary doctorates. She is the only writer of children's books to have been awarded a MacArthur Fellowship.

Ms. Hamilton is married to Arnold Adoff, who is a distinguished poet and anthologist.

About This Point Signature Author

VIRGINIA HAMILTON is one of the most distinguished writers of our time. Winner of the National Book Award and the Hans Christian Andersen Medal, she is the author of *M. C. Higgins, the Great*, winner of the Newbery Medal, as well as *Sweet Whispers, Brother Rush; The Planet of Junior Brown;* and *In the Beginning*, all Newbery Honor Books. Her books of folklore include *The People Could Fly*, winner of the Coretta Scott King Award; and *Many Thousand Gone*. Ms. Hamilton has also written the novel *Plain City*, an ALA Notable Book and a *School Library Journal* Best Book; *Jaguarundi*, a picture book; *Her Stories: African American Folktales, Fairy Tales, and True Tales*, winner of the Coretta Scott King Award, an ALA Notable Book, a BBYA, a *Booklist* Editors' Choice, a *School Library Journal* Best Book of the Year, and an NCTE Notable Children's Book in the Language Arts; and *When Birds Could Talk & Bats Could Sing*, a *School Library Journal* Best Book of the Year, an *American Bookseller* Pick of the Lists, an ALA Notable Book, and a *BCCB* Blue Ribbon Book. Most recently she is the author of *A Ring of Tricksters: Animal Tales from America, the West Indies, and Africa*. She has been awarded the 1995 Laura Ingalls Wilder Medal as well as four honorary doctorates. She is the only writer of children's books to have been awarded a MacArthur Fellowship.

Ms. Hamilton is married to Arnold Adoff, who is a distinguished poet and anthologist.